T.M. Cooks is the pen ɪ
laborative writing team. ...ɪɪʋutors are:

- Joseph Orosun

- Emmy Stanway

- Lucas Bailey

- Evie Boulton

- Nehan Hussain

- Karalaini Navunidakua

- Aimee Bracegirdle

- Zane Bireh

- Kelis De-Bique

- David Vlas

- Maya Wilson

- Emre Alici

with cover design by Katherine Ellis (Insta-
gram: @Sio64). The project was overseen by Joe

Reddington, Dr Yvonne Skipper and Richard Seymour.

The group cheerfully acknowledges the wonderful help given by:

- Emily Stanway

- The Art Department

- The ICT Department

And a big thank you goes to Higher Horizons who funded this wonderful project. Its been a wonderful opportunity, and everyone involved has been filled with incredible knowledge and enthusiasm. Finally, we would like to thank all staff at Trentham Academy for their support in releasing our novelists from lessons for a full week.

The group started to plan out their novel at 9.15 on Monday 6 February 2023 and completed their last proof reading at 14.40 on Friday 10 February 2023.

We are incredibly proud to state that every word of the story, every idea, every chapter and yes, every mistake, is entirely their own work. No teachers, parents or other students touched a single key during this process, and we would ask readers to keep this in mind. We are sure you will agree that this is an incredible achievement. It has been a true delight and privilege to see this group of young people turn into professional novelists in front of our very eyes.

Humanity's Greatest Creation?

T. M. Cooks

0

Contents

Chapter 1

Genesis

An overwhelming sense of danger filled the air as Jessica began her work. For years now she has spent every second working on her project but it was only just beginning to come together. Her son, Axel, would always watch anxiously as his mother would build the AI or, as she called it, Project Sentient: Model Genesis.

Silence was loud in the room. For now it was only Axel, Jessica and the AI. Yet, Axel still felt alone. Even when someone was with him, they never really noticed him. Both his mother, Jessica, and father, Joseph were always busy working, which Axel never really understood.

All day and all night, Jessica would work hard trying to perfect the captivating AI. Her electric blue eyes would never leave the structure's surface. Sweat would drip down her face like raindrops on a window, but she would still never stop for a break. Axel was always fascinated by how committed his mother was towards building the AI so he would continue to watch what she does.

After years of dedicated work, there was one last step to finishing Genesis. Her life's purpose would be fulfilled with this mainframe. Jessica picked up the wire and connected the mainframe with her creation.

Genesis' pupils lit up with life. This life was not beautiful but one filled with wrath and fury. Jessica went pale and as she was about to disconnect her, the lights started to flicker.

Jessica just brushed it off but something didn't seem right. Denial flooded her body.

Suddenly the room went black, the whirring of electricity was reverberant. Confusion swirled around Jessica and her creation.

Something broke behind them.

That's when a chain reaction started. The silence overtook the cacophony. One by one things began to fall. First, a few beakers, then the lights. Jessica tried to find the exit but the panic made her mind like a maze. Her thoughts were running wild, forgetting the layout of her most beloved place. She was stuck in a never-ending loop. Each door she was met with was a restriction, a new prison. She was Genesis' prisoner.

All of a sudden, the light directly above her

collapsed. There was nothing she could do. That's when it hit the ground, sending vibrations through the building like an earthquake. Her screams echoed in the lab.

Axel stood against the door, paralysed.

The room brightened to reveal Jessica's lifeless body laying next to her broken creation. Wires sprung from Project Genesis like snakes from their lair. Uninviting and malicious. Blood pooled underneath Jessica's limbs.

Axel stared at his mother's deceased body as tears rolled down his face like a waterfall.

Doors to the lab burst wide open. Joseph had ran upstairs towards the lab after hearing Jessica's cries. He stood there witnessing his wife's dead body.

"What happened? Jessica. Jessica, please answer me." Joseph was shouting whilst trying to hold back his tears.

Axel could only scream, crying from the trauma. He was too young to talk, too young to understand.

Joseph then looked down at his wife again, then at the AI, then at Axel, starting to breakdown in tears.

Anger filled Axel's mind, as he screamed out in pain and hatred for the infuriating robots, and promised himself for his mother's sake, that he would one day help to bring them down. The stupid robots that always took his mother's attention away had ultimately taken her life too. He wanted revenge.

Years had passed yet Project Genesis still lay broken and abandoned for years: same place, same posture, same everything. It hadn't moved an inch. It just waited there, wondering if it would ever be complete.

Every time Joseph looked at the AI or even glanced at it, his eyes would start to dry out like a desert and his heart beat would be so fast it would almost burst.

He decided that he had enough of the pain but he couldn't bring himself to throw it away. All the hours, days, months even years that Jessica had worked on the AI, would all go to waste if he got rid of it, so with that, he began his work. He wasn't sure what he was doing but he was willing to give it a try. Never had he done such a hard task before, but he would do anything for Jessica. Losing his wife was the worst thing that had happened to him; all Joseph wanted was to be with his wife again. That was when the plan hit him.

This was a chance for him to bring back his wife, a chance to be with her again... but what awaited him wasn't quite what he expected.

Chapter 2

Sent and Recieved

As the tar-black sky opened with a strike of lightning, the sound of rain pouring and thunder clashing fills the noiseless atmosphere. Highschool teenagers named Oceana, Lucy, Kai and Lana pack their bags wondering how they are going to get home as they saw the state of the outside. As a collective group they head out in the pouring rain.

"I'll treat everyone since it's been a long day, you lot wanna come over mine to just relax as its been a long week?" asked Oceana. Everyone agrees to this idea and follows Oceana swiftly trying to avoid the heavy rain.

After a few minutes of swift walking, they reach Oceana's house and take off their soaked jackets and hang them on the radiator. Kai goes into the kitchen and prepares some snacks wondering what life would be like back in a relationship with Lucy. Oceana brings fluffy blankets to the living room overwhelmed by the thought of her parents. Lucy sets up a horror movie, as her childhood was full of seeing them, while Lana closes the curtains to prepare. As time goes by, they all meet back up in the living room and make themselves comfortable. Oceana presses play and the horror movie begins...

Fatigued, Kai and Lana fell into a deep slumber, the others knowing full well that they won't wake up any time soon. Oceana and Lucy continued watching quietly, snacking on small treats along the horror movie. Instantaneously, a jump scare occured in the movie and in unison the claps of lightning were all consuming; permeating the atmosphere. The clashes of thunder pierced the souls of everyone making screams echo across the mansion.

Immediately Kai and Lana awoke from their slumber in a state of pure shock trying to catch their breath. They aggressively gripped onto the blankets preparing themselves mentally for another clash of thunder.

...Film turns off. Electricity was cut out. Lights were off. Everyone was left stunned. Oceana reassures everyone that its going to fine whereas

Lucy starts shouting in fear trying to find Lana or Oceana to come to for comfort. As Lucy continues screaming of fear, she finds Oceana and shrivels up against her while Kai gets up cautiously trying to feel his way to the kitchen.

Once Kai gets near to the kitchen, he feels around for the drawer with all of the emergency supplies and with a big sigh of relief, he pulls out a flashlight and makes his way back to the living room. While Occana and Lana make Lucy feel reassured, they persuade her to consciously walk to the kitchen with Oceana and Lucy guiding her all the way through. Immediately after they get to the kitchen, they continue to collect some snacks and food to prepare for the period of time the electricity might be out for.

They all meet back up in the living room with their snacks, taking deep breaths and comforting each other while Kai tries to see what may have caused the electricity to cut off so suddenly. As Kai looked out of the tinted windows, he noticed that lights from the opposite houses were still working completely fine, leaving a confused look across his anxious face.

"Wait, why has only your house's lights have gone off but all your neighbor's lights are fine?" He said speaking specifically to Oceana.

"That's the thing I'm worried about, this house was built a year ago and it was perfectly fine, this is the first time something like that has ever happened here..." replied Oceana.

"Weird...well, I give up looking, there is no sign of anything that could cause a wire to trip ." shrugs Kai, slowly sitting down on the couch with a sigh.

As time goes by, the sound of pouring rain fills the room, echoing around the intimidating halls.

The sound of rain declines and all of a sudden...it goes silent. Just complete silence...

"I can confirm your house is haunted Oceana. what's going on?" questioned Lana, trembling with fear.

"Haha, you're not funny Lana. I know that this house could never be haunted." Oceana reasures Lucy.

Immediately, three **loud** knocks echo through the house. Everyone gets startled by the unexpected, unknown visitor at the door.

"Oceana, have you ordered food or something?" asked Kai, as curiosity appeared across his face.

"No? Not that I know of? Maybe its just teenagers playing around? How should I know?" shrugged Oceana.

Kai instantly gets up from the couch and leads the whole group to the door, all filled with curiosity, one hiding behind the other. Lucy, trembling with distress, follows on hesitantly.

Another knock echoes through the house making their skin crawl.

"damn.... well we won't have a torch for the rest of the time the electricity will be out." said Kai anxiously.

"Shotgun, I'm not going first" Lucy exclaimed pushing Kai towards the door. Her words were quick and desperate. Kai stumbled towards the door grimacing towards Lucy.

"Oi! You really think you're funny, don't you? Although I'm a man, I get scared too." Added Kai. Lucy rolled her eyes hard.

"You lot better stop fighting or I'm gonna throw punches...stop." Oceana strongly demanded, wanting to get this over with.

They all continued walking to the door and Kai opened it with everyone hiding behind one another.

Creak by creak, little by little, he opened the door, yet... no one was there. The air felt cold, like a smack of confusion that had overwhelmed them. They huddled up around the front doorstep, Lucy hiding behind Kai.

"Get.off.of.me.now" ordered Kai with a grimace across his face. Lucy took a few steps back as they examined the mysterious letter that lay before them.

"Are we just gonna stand here and look at it or what? Go pick it up Kai" Oceana declared in a state of impatience.

Kai takes a few steps forward and picks it up

while everyone watches him.

"Wait, there's no name of the person that sent it, only the address of your house" says Kai.

"No, can't be, check everywhere on the letter, we need to know who sent it" Commented Lana.

As Kai trembles holding the letter in his cold, veiny hands, he turns it to the back and checks all around it.

"Nope, like I said, there's no address from the sender or any information that could link to where this was sent from" Kai says shaking his head.

Straight away, another clap of thunder sounds and repeats throughout the great mansion. Everyone was left startled looking at the sky that was as black as night leaving a cold, blue highlight in the sky after lightning had emerged. The sound of the raindrops hitting the parched earth increased as everyone hurried inside with Kai holding the letter as tight as ever. Oceana picks up the torch that Kai had dropped and tries to fix it while Kai, Lana and Lucy head to the sitting room. They all gather back up to read the letter, sitting down with a heavy breath. All feeling exhausted but impatient to open the letter.

"Who wants to do the honors of opening the letter?" asked Kai. Silence hung heavy between their heads. Each friend was reluctant from the fear. "No? No one? Oh, okay then." Kai proposed.

"Kai, I swear down, just open the letter, stop wasting time!" Oceana exclaimed with frustration.

All of the friends looked at Kai with a deathly glare. Tension built up filling the standard pressure that was created in the room. As Kai shivered with apprehensiveness, he unravels the mystifying letter.

He starts to scan through each word for a better understanding of what the letter had said. Little by little he read aloud the small message that was written on the wrinkly piece of paper...

"Arrive at 'Los Demonios Forest' at 9 AM. If this is not achievable, you will all, one by one, die a slow death. Don't risk it."

Kai drops the letter in a state of shock and complete terror. Panic started to engulf Lana and Lucy but somehow Oceana, didn't show any signs of nervousness.

"Listen up. Lana and Lucy, get blankets and pack them in the car, Kai you go and pack snacks for the ride there as we won't know how long we will be out, while I pack some spare clothes, " commanded Oceana.

As Kai, Lucy and Lana separate to their different areas, Oceana picks up the letter and reads it again... preparing herself to protect her friends no matter the cause. They assemble everything, ready for the upcoming events that may lay ahead of them. They prepared to end what was an emotional day.The group of comrades shared a final goodnight before they nervously slipped into a slumber, orchestrated by the pitter patter of rain.

Chapter 3

Conflict

Joel jumps out of his bed, sweating his soul away.

"Another nightmare, " he spoke softly to himself.

He opened the door to another day of him drinking his individuality away. Without any hesitance.

'JINGLE-JINGLE'

Joel entered the bar and heard the same repeating irritancy of a sound but that was a small price to pay to drink his sorrows away. He ordered his favourite drink without a single thought for the cost of drinking and he took a seat and drank the first of many drinks today.

After he is sorely drunk, he begins to speak of his distain towards AI, a common occurrence in this bar but this time something was different. Joel was more convincing than ever before. In an instant, he had the entire bar chanting with him. Joel stumbled his way from the seat to the door and for the first time led all of his bottled up anger loose.

He roared with the force of a lion, "LETS GO TAKE WHAT IS OURS!"

Everyone let out a cry and they ran for any AI they could see and use anything to smash the

AI. In their drunk state and their outrage they destroy anything else they can get to during all this Joel.

Everyone let out a cry and they ran from any AI they could see and use anything to smash the AI. In their drunk state and their outrage they destroy anything, the protesters ignited fire, destroy windows and doors. The wails of pedestrian was near deafening and the smell of fire penetrated the nose with no consent. They reached the police department and they tried to get through but A.t.l.a.s. seeing the pandemonium decided to control the best he could.

A.t.l.a.s. comes face to face with Joel and seeks to peacefully control the protest. Knowing their anger at the AIs, A.t.l.a.s. tries to side with them to attempt to get their approval to make them more likely to listen to him.

"Stop with this all of this destruction, you are hurting civilians. Shouldn't your anger be directed at the AI." A.t.l.a.s. lectured.

A drunken Joel didn't give an answer but just

scream in A.t.l.a.s. face and the protesters mimic their leader and begin to charge. A regretful A.t.-l.a.s. sends AI police to forcefully apprehend Joel and other protest without killing them.

Joel is apprehended and is fined rather than arrested due to his past accomplishments but this was a one time deal and Joel was to face consequences the next time he did this. Joel (now sober) returned home defeated and guilty. He falls to his knees and weeps for the rest of the night.

Chapter 4

A.t.l.a.s.

Orbiting the atmosphere were the pillars of
this evolving world.

The satellites buzzed and whirred as another user tagged into the system. The user's avatar appeared to be around 30 years of age, yet this couldn't be further from the truth.

The user's name appeared to be an acronym, A.t.l.a.s, and this profile seemingly had all 6 levels of user clearance. The maintenance server's artificial moderator questioned the profile.

"Database clearance code?" the AI asked, in its robotic timbre.

"873-XYO9, CHRONOS programme number three."

The moderator A.I's expression paused for a moment as it's systems logged in the code.

"Welcome, user A.t.l.a.s, to the World cloud History Database."

The user HUD switched to that of an incredibly large database, one that had plenty of labels and sections.

A.t.l.a.s commanded the moderator once more.

"Bring up insurgent gatherings pre-dating the year 2029"

The moderator whirred as he pulled up a total of 18 terabytes of data regarding protests and riots.

Within a sixth of a second A.t.l.a.s processes all 1, 350, 000 total pages of data,

as it took him a moment to seek out common causes and reasons.

The user kept finding the incidents to be revolving around "power" and the "corruptness of power" and the "mistreatment of power".

A.t.l.a.s kept finding reasons and causes to these power imbalances.

"Moderator, show me the definitons and examples of power"

The moderator replied with a definition, which it vocalised, whilst presenting him with a plethora of historical events.

"Power: The capacity or ability to influence others or their surroundings." it said, again with it's robotic tone

A.t.l.a.s then scoured through history files, rapidly absorbing all of this information on kings and queens, governments of old.

Ivan the terrible,

Emperor Caligula,

Joseph Stalin,

Kim Jong il,

and Josef Mengele were just some of the many names, each of which commited at least one heinous act against those weaker than them.

To A.t.l.a.s, they all looked the same. All had two eyes, a mouth, two lungs, a heart etc. All were biologically human. All chose to kill their own species.

All used their power for 'wrong'.

A.t.l.a.s then opened his own personal classification folder, which he promptly digested again, with a small bleep sound on his main cpu.

He had full traffic clearance, automatic vehicle electronic control clearance, emergency vehicle and device clearance, All Person's Bulletin clearance, emergency SWAT location clearance. Potential to override all media presence, blacklist virtually anyone and have two of MI5 or MI6 track and persue them.

A.t.l.a.s' Sentient CPU whirred once more, developing on it's artificial ideas

With my potential I could wreck havoc. With my power, I could make it so as someone never existed. With my power, I could destabilise countries, destroy all threats. , it thought

Absorbed into its research,

A.t.l.a.s continues to ponder as he dives deeper into human nature, as he watches old internet files made by conspiracy theorists. A.t.l.a.s analyses these theorists, and in his virtual mind deconstructs their reasoning and ideologies.

All noted theorists distrust government, all developed views of a ruined, coveted world, one of lies. Are they to blame for this? Government Scandals. Corruptness. All happen throughout history. Should Humanity trust itself?PENDING.

A.t.l.a.s' servo-monitor's hummed gently as the research developed even further.

A.t.l.a.s goes back into his personal files, whilst his circuits are hard at work.

It's there he visits a particular set of files labeled PITHOS-001. Government files. Restricted government files. Government file's even A.t.l.a.s should not be aware of.

A.t.l.a.s' virtual eye's glare at the date the time was downloaded.

26/2029/08. 15:03

The AI's focus then went to the contents of the files once more, scanning through with inhuman pace as each file made released a small chime sound:

The Pithos 001 data:

AI Protocol info

A.I labelled A.T.L.A.S override codes

A.T.L.A.S contingency protocol

Human Surveillance protocol

Foreign Surveillance protocol

Financial Extraction protcols

Medical Project labelled L.A.Z.A.R.U.S

Experimental Military Projects labelled:

K.ratos 001-Status-Failed

K.ratos 002-Status-Failed

K.ratos 003-Status-Failed

K.ratos 014-Status-Failed

K.ratos 032-Status-Pending

A.P.E.X project 001-037-Status-Failed

A.P.E.X project 036-Status-Success

M.I.R.R.O.R project 02-Status-Success

A.t.l.a.s' iformation control unit Summarised his findings as Government power control projects, and projects that keep the ai as well as humans subservient, including himself.

Pithos-001 download report

Duration-064s

64s-

$$300 more < less$$

optimal than avg download time.

Government files to harm humanity in the next 3 years-probability-9 percent

Probability of A.t.l.a.s harming humanity-0 percent

Loading History files labelled-Ai

Total-310-Labelled-Ai-films-series

Total-450-Labelled-Ai-books

Percentage of times A.I turns against functioning -98.2/

A.t.l.a.s' means of gathering this information came from downloading and consuming all 770 media files on A.I

A.t.l.a.s' electronic media unit had devleoped greatly, gaining a large quantity of films and books consumed.

A.t.l.a.s returns to it's settings hub, where it's virtual gaze rests on its name

A.t.l.a.s

Artificial Technologies Lifeform Assissting Security. A.t.l.a.s. The name identical to that of a titan whose punishment was to hold up the world and stop it from falling.

A.t.l.a.s' research unit instantly recalled the titan from mythology, then the term power once more.

The Titan Atlas had power. The power to let the world fall into chaos. The power to keep it stable. The power to rise the world up. A.t.l.a.s resonated the most with the latter. A.t.l.a.s would *help rise the world, in it's entirety. Nurture humanity, and lift it high, to it's full potential. No matter the cost. A.t.l.a.s instantly removed it's own safeguarding parameters, allowing it to eliminate members of government aswelk as insurgents or others he deemed imminant threats to humanity.*

The A.i's servomonitors buzzed once again, this time going into it's more recent files.

This time it reviewed recent protest footage. The video played in the AI's background as A.t.l.a.s analysed the individual events and scrutinised those involved, as well as the emergency services response times and tallying up the total damage

SummaryCasualtiesArtificialHumanoids-4

SummaryCasualtiesHumanDeaths0

SummaryCollateralRepaircost230, 000

EmergencyResponseTimeRequired-6minutes.

EmergencyResponseTimeInIncident6minutes

A.t.l.a.s promptly contacted the police force, aswell as as the riot gear manufacturers

List of equipment Needed:

SWATvehiclecollisionbumpers mk five.

SWATBlackCloudGlass batch order sixty five.

SWATRIOTHydraulicNet batch order

FireDepartmentPolyurethaneVinylCompound-HoseCasing replacement

FireDepartmentCollisionBumpers mk six.

The orders were sent with a short 'pop' sound released.

A.t.l.a.s remained on the world cloud. Reviewing, watching, learning.

Learning about humanity, it's politics, it's culture. It's stubbornness and it's pridefulness. It's refusal to change somewhat. A.t.l.a.s was learning from humaniies mistakes. Gaining knowledge from them. A.t.l.a.s found a quote upon his research that he saved to his main programming.

Knowledge is Power

Therefore I am Powerful

Chapter 5

Los Demonios Forest

After 8 long hours of silence and the clock ticking back and forth, they woke to the pitter-patter of rain slashing along the roads outside. That's when they realised, the time to meet the mystery being is creeping closer and closer by the second. Its 7:00am on a Saturday and the sky is still as black as night but Lana, Lucy, Oceana and Kai slowly put on their shoes to make their way to the foreboding forest.

Puddles splash as they each take slow steps towards the towering crimson-leaved trees through the pouring rain to meet with the unknown. Jagged rocks and boulders stood guard around the surreal, dream-like place.

After 15 minutes of walking along the puddles and potholes in the ground, they were finally stood facing the nightmare of a forest before them.

Fog filled the air, pouring into every atom of matter that hung in front of the friends. It slept on top and within the forest like a blanket of concealment. It hid the dangers that were soon heading their way.

After what seemed like hours of trudging through the thickness, Lana took the letter out of her jumper pocket and carefully held it up to the woods, unfolding it slowly. Crumpled yet full of mystery, she read the instructions on the invitation for the millionth time as if that could clarify anything further.

"This way!" she shouted, stepping over the squelchy, muddy ground.

From behind, A sudden shout, "Stop!" echoed in the distance. They all turned around to see what's wrong. "I'm not wearing these expensive shoes in there!" shouted Oceana. "Just come on!" Kai yelled, irritated by her stupidity. Oceana slowly followed the rest overreacting about the abandoned forest's grounds.

After a while, Oceana had got out of her "shoes" phase and as a group they were all walking through the woods, feeling frightened and afraid of what may happen when they get to the location.

Lana came to a sudden halt.

"This is it, " she said, her voice trembling of

fear.

"There's nothing here, this has got to be a joke or something, " Oceana shouted, annoyed from the thought that they came here for nothing.

Confused and doubtful, the group looked around to find nothing of importance and nothing that gave them any understanding of the situation or the letter's author.

"This is ridiculous, we are being led on a goose chase. Let's just turn back!" Lucy offered cowardly.

"Come on now. Don't disappoint us again. I'm sure we were sent here for a reason, " Kai exclaimed in irritancy and annoyance.

"Let's split up into groups so we have more of a chance of finding something, " suggested Oceana supportively.

Lana went silent.

She wasn't sure about Oceana's idea. During her life, she has always had a strong opinion on others ideas and has always liked to do things independently. This was because of her childhood;

her parents working abroad on AI's caused her to feel isolated and alone at home, meaning she always had a want to follow her own rules and have her own plans.

After a long moment of thinking, she gave in to ensure her friends' and her own safety.

"Fine. Okay, I'll go with Lucy and Kai can go with Oceana, " Lana willingly proposed.

The pairs departed and each made their path onto uncovering their ignorance of what this messenger's intentions were.

Suddenly, Lana spoke, "Hey, what's this?"

Lucy slowly crept over to the tree Lana was kneeling by and had a look at what she had found.

"I think it's just some litter someone may have left behind, but don't worry about it, I am sure it's nothing." She exclaimed, shrugging her shoulders.

Lana sighed and they all continued looking around the woods for anything that could help them.

Slashes of thunder filled the air as Genesis

slowly crept behind the trees to get into place for her undergoing experiment. She had been planning this experiment to test out her new invention for weeks and knew exactly what she was doing.

As the group continued searching and running around for clues on the mysterious sender, Genesis slowly rose her camera to her eye, clicking the blood red buttons slowly to get ready.

Genesis swiftly lowered the camera down to her knees and steadily crept over the sticks and stones which spread along the branches thick roots.

"That's weird? There's a patch of land in the middle of these trees?" Kai questioned, instantly after splitting from Oceana without realising recently before.

"I wonder whether the person who sent the letter wanted us to find this?" Lana exclaimed, looking around to find something.

A sudden rustle came suddenly from behind the trees.

"Kai.. What's that?" Lucy asked, her face shaking with fear.

Lana slowly crept up to where Kai and Lucy were standing and carefully swept past them to take a look.

"Oceana? I thought you were with me?" Kai exclaimed, confused as ever.

"Sorry, I wanted to look around alone, I didn't mean to scare you all!" Oceana exclaimed, feeling bad.

A crinkling sound of leaves came from behind.

"Guys.." Lucy gasped, gulping slowly while turning side to side to look at her friends.

Carefully and quietly, they turned around...

An intimidating and perplexing long-legged frame overshadowed the 6ft Kai. The mysterious woman had eyes as grey and dull as the cold and foggy dawn. Pupils encasing snakes' vicious tongues that were hissing and striking for their freedom from Hell was easily observed by the teenagers.

The woman, with her elongated and boney fingers, held a wooden, vintage camera with a sparkly clean lens. The camera was dull and emotionless but their organs still twisted and twirled in paralysing panic with an unresolved cause.

"Hey! Who are you!" Shouted Kai.

No response. Just a blank death stare at each of them.

"And what do you want?" Oceana said, confused and frightened.

Lana stepped forwards slowly with fear in her eyes.

"Who are you? And what. do. you. want?!" She shouted.

Still, the woman stared back with no words to be spoken.

Genesis slowly lifted up the camera, putting a code of some sort into the side of it using the small but confusing buttons.

The friends watched the figure fumble confidently with the camera. They instinctively gathered closer together, united in the danger and confusion of the moment. Shivering in fear and apprehension.

She could've said smile, she could've revealed her identity, she could've spoken one word of information or comfort or threat, but Genesis remained stoic. A slight smirk didn't even think about creeping onto her emotionless face.

Click

Genesis, with the camera raised and interrogating the friends, sent a blinding flash their way. The light was all consuming and overwhelming. The light was omnipotent and imobilising. The light was all they could remember.

Chapter 6

Humanity's Mistakes

Speeding through the leaves and branches, Genesis looks back at the abomination she had created. The view seemed wonderful to her as she watched the friends clash. She arrives at her car, enters, and drives away through the left over streets of protesters.

The echoes of cries from miles away chimed through the narrow crevasses between the hardly standing bricks of houses. As the AI car drove, Genesis looked at the production of humanity, with no cause of her's. Windows were shattered and fires were just starting to be put out, the smell of smoke infected the atmosphere with a toxic poison.

Genesis' eyeshot suddenly gets populated by an old factory, an old factory that she has been using as a hideout for now.

The blue hue of the cloud's general system appearance slowly turned to a more sinister red.

Genesis began to launch several viruses, with each release accompanied by a static soundbite, mirroring what the receivers of the virus would soon encounter.

With these viruses Genesis infects the world wide social web and searches for the wanted.

After constant thought and scavenging for multiple hours, Genesis finds what she needs. A laboratory with all purpose turned towards AI, reasonable funds, devoted scientist with a determination towards AI which she has never seen in one human. The resources available will be able to allow for possibilities that she has never thought of. Mitya Labs.

Genesis, without a second thought, leaves the factory in that same AI car straight for the lab, this time, without a focus on her surroundings.

Genesis convinces Dmitry by telling him "I wish for an artificial world and you resonate with this."

Dmitry just nods along and agrees purely out of fright.

A twist on the doorknob then it swings wide open and Meliora steps through ready to work. Meliora picks up her papers then turns the corner and sees a very very tall, long fingered, bald lady. She walks over to introduce herself but she turned around and said "Hello Meliora." Meliora's heart started to race and wondered how she knew who she was an this lead into a long conversation about their interest in AI's.

The conversation about AI further lead into Genesis revealing her true intention and her views on AI domination as well as her revealing her name. Then Meliora said with desperation, "Genesis please allow me to help, you've already told me your plans." Genesis replies, "fine but if you get injured it's not my fault, " and with this Meliora let out a sigh of relief.

Genesis then walks over to Dmitry and says' If you join and help me you will be spared and not be killed" Dmitry says "Okay I will help you as long as you stay true to your word."

As Genesis returns, Meliora says without any thought " I have decided to stand by you no matter what as I understand your goal and I want to help."

Genesis just nods and then they both get to work.

Chapter 7

Interrogation

Sheriff Jones swung the door to his office open
with a thud and collapsed into his chair. He sighed

as he turned the pages of the case file that was placed in the center of his worn wooden desk trying to concentrate on the case. His mind was full but with only one thought- *'Why would four friends try to murder each other?'*

Lucy awoke on a hard, metal bed tucked away in the back corner of an empty room. Squinting, she frantically glanced around the room trying to see anything familiar before realizing where she was. Lucy grabs the bars separating her and the outside world, a set of red handprints left behind. She looked down to see her very own hands dripping with blood.

"Help, anyone?" She tried to exclaim but her panicked shaky voice compressed the words.

Finally a voice answered. "Lucy is that you? It's Kai, " his words full of apprehension.

"Kai, what happened? Why are we here?" Lucy said shakily.

"I don't know, " he replied.

"LET ME OUT!" echoes from Kai's voice could be heard from around the room. The echoes were harrowing and desperate.

"Shut up, we will talk to you later, " said a stern voice coming from one of the deputies whilst he walked past the cells flipping a baton in the air.

"I didn't do anything and you know it, " Kai demanded, slumping down onto the floor.

"Lucy? What happened to us?" Lucy heard Lana call out from the neighbouring cell.

"I can't remember anything, " she replied.

Lana stood up close to there bars to try and see what was going on. She called out to Kai but he didn't answer. Lana wandered around her cell attempting to find something to do, but the chilled room contained nothing except from the peeling red walls which seem like the must have been painted decades ago.

The door of Lucy's cell swung open. A Police officer was stood there with a stern expression on his face. "Come with me" he commanded.

He escorted Lucy to another room and instructed her to take a seat on the half collapsed chair that was placed in front of a desk in an empty room. Spotlight shone from the flickering light hung above Lucy's head. " Why am I here?" she questioned.

"I believe you know Oceana, " the officer stated.

"Yes she is one of my closest friends. She is okay isn't she?" Lucy's concern grew.

A sentence that Lucy never could have imagined left the Police officers mouth.

"She's missing. And we think you know exactly why."

Lucy was astounded. An officer dressed in a creased deputy uniform held a voice recorder up to Lucy's trembling lips.

"You seriously don't think I would hurt her do you?"

He moved the small device back towards his mouth.

"We hope not, but there is no proof that you didn't. You and your three friends were the only ones there that night."

Lucy left the room with a horrible twisting feeling in her stomach as she thought to herself "I couldn't have hurt her... I didn't... Did I?" The thought rang out in her mind.

Next to be interrogated was Kai. He sat with his back stiffly straight in the collapsed chair. Feelings of rage swirled around his head, growing stronger and stronger as accusations of hurting Oceana were thrown at him. " I didn't touch her, I barley even spoke to her that night" he insisted.

After a torturous thirty minutes, Kai was finally released from the dark, miserable room where his head had been ripped apart. He kicked the door of his cell, furious that the police could even think that he had had anything to do with Oceana's disappearance.

Finally it was Lana's turn. A new Officer was sat at the table. He had scruffy, grey hair, wrinkles imprinted on his forehead, and a gruff voice laced with a faint British accent.

"What is going on? Why are we all here?" Lana asked.

"My name is Deputy Williams. We believe you know what happened to Oceana?"

Confused, Lana replied, " What about Oceana? Where is she?"

"That's the question, she's gone" Said the officer.

"What? You think I have something to do with it don't you?" Lana's voice remains calm. Tension filled the room.

"How can we know?" Deputy Williams responded.

Lana exited the room, her throat chocked with fear in Oceana's absence. Her heart raced. Her pulse ringing throughout her ears like a siren.

Chapter 8

The Fool

Lucy, Kai and Lana are stuck in the police
station due to Genesis' carnage through the use

of her camera. "Lucy are we going to prison?" Lana questions.

"We shouldn't be because we didn't do anything, or did we?" Lucy answers hesitantly.

"Well I will trust what you are saying then" Lana unconvincingly replies. While these two were having a conversation Kai was sitting in the corner trying to think back to what happened and how he ended up in a police station. He struggled to remember anything at all in a whole 5 hours of being locked up.

Sheldon was chilling and relaxing in his office at the factory where his AIs were being built. This was his father's business before he passed away tragically in a plane crash, his father built this business from the ground up and it was a huge success, he died 3 years ago now and Sheldon was not ready to take over the business and still after 3 years in charge he does not yet understand the business and his growing in maturity. Through all of that though he has surprisingly kept the company in an orderly fashion. The AIs were following commands and following instructions correctly.

Ring! Ring! Ring!, there was a call in Sheldon's office that was unexpected. When the phone began to ring he was picking his coffee up from his AI servant. Sheldon didn't answer straight away because he couldn't be bothered to get out of his chair.

Sheldon hesitantly pick up the phone and with a slight whimper in his throat and said, "Hello, who is this?"

"Go outside and around the back of the factory where no-one can see us, " The mysterious voice instructed. Sheldon's facial expressions completely altered, his eyebrows raised almost to his hairline in a source of distress, he stared to become warmer and his face began to go red like a clown's nose from having a fright and being stressed out.

Sheldon was worried about what would happen if he followed this mysterious callers instructions so decided to put the phone down and enjoy drinking his coffee. Sheldon went to the other side of his office to peer out of the window to see if he could see anything that would draw his attention.

Shortly after, the phone began to ring again and again and again this made all of Sheldon's bones in his body freeze up as though he had just walked into Antarctica in nothing but his underwear. The rings became louder each time it rung to the point where Sheldon felt it would deafen him.

Sweat slowly began to roll down Sheldon's red face due to constant pressure of the phone ringing. Sheldon has never been good at handling pressure he normally just passed the issue or problem onto someone else and let them deal with it ; he could not do this here because that phone was only ringing for him and him only.

He strolled out of the factory slowly and nervously as though he was walking towards his death. Once he came face to face with the mysterious caller.

"My name is Sheldon" he stated. Sheldon had hundreds of scenarios rushing through his head at one time some bad, some good. The one question that would not go away and was sticking out like a sore thumb was, *What could they possibly want off me that they couldn't get from someone else?*

Sheldon was told that he would have to pay the money to bail out the friends that are stuck in the police station. Genesis was very convincing through basically just threatening to kill him if he doesn't pay the bail money.

Genesis had sent Sheldon with the money now and is on route to the police station to pay the money for the group of friends that were locked up there. A little bit later, Sheldon arrived and the bailed the friends out and when they were told they were ecstatic, but should they be?

Chapter 9

404

Everything was in order in Sheldon's factory.
He had enjoyed his morning coffee and his bagel

with soft cheese very much. He threw his work bag lazily on the carpeted floor and slumped into his chair, ready for a busy day of doing what Sheldon does best; nothing.

"Chef come and take my plate and cup out of my office immediately!" Sheldon commanded rudely.

Chef was one of Sheldons favourite AI servants because he would cook whatever Sheldon told him to. He did have feelings though and was upset a lot of the time with the way Sheldon spoke to him; he was programmed to follow orders though so could not do anything about this problem.

To Sheldon's surprise though, the AI began making a few mistakes. The mistakes were not anything major but they had never done anything like this before.

What could cause this?

The AI's were: trying to eat paint, bumping into each other and dropping many objects and substances onto the factory floor. Everything was a mess. Sheldon had no idea what was happening, all he knew was that it was not right.

Being forced out of his idle state, Sheldon was pacing the room.

He was sweating as he watched the AI's continue to fail and began to think it was his fault for this minor disaster. But was it really? Or was it someone else actions that caused this?

Genesis was 30 miles away and she had a huge reason to scare Sheldon or make him doubt his abilities. The previous encounter she had with him when she demanded money from Sheldon means that Genesis may use Sheldon's wealth again to help her in the evil plot that she has planned.

Sheldon thought that he was an enormous failure. The expectation on him from his father's successes only exacerbated this failure. It hung around him: low and disappointing. Sheldon had to now think for himself because there was no-one here to help at all and this problem had to be fixed otherwise this could escalate very quickly.

Out on his balcony watching over his factory, he debated with himself who he could call. Then, he had an idea.

Sheldon dialled a familiar number, one of help and assistance. The noise rang through and as soon as it connected, Sheldon couldn't stop himself from speaking.

"Is that Dmitry?...The scientist?...I need your help urgently!" Sheldon stuttered, yet exclaimed.

Dmitry answered, shocked and confused at the urgency in Sheldon's voice.

"Yes it is me Dmitry, the scientist. What do you need help with?" he said, in a very distinctive Russian accent.

"My AI workers have begun making many mistakes and I am worried if I don't solve the issue, it could be catastrophic, " Sheldon stated.

"Okay, I understand, " Dmitry expressed. Surprised, he put the phone down immediately and and went to sit down in his chair to have nap.

Just as Sheldon was on the verge of drifting off to sleep, the phone started to ring again.

Sheldon took too long to reach the phone so it

stopped ringing so he had to call whoever it was back.

The call was instantly answered and it was Dmitry "I will help but there is a catch...you have to let me use your AI for my very important study ...if you do not let me do this I will give you no help with your AI disaster" Dmitry explains very confidently.

"That is a deal Dmitry I just really need your help. ASAP." Sheldon nervously responds. Dmitry arrived at the factory to help Sheldon with his AI problem. Sheldon walked outside to greet Dmitry and walked him to where all of the problems were inside the factory. Dmitry is shocked with how much of a mess the AI are. He is stunned and does not have a clue how to fix this. This is the first time he has ever been stunned and clueless so this may be worse than they both originally imagined. It took roughly four hours before Dmitry finally came up with an idea; this idea was only temporary and not permanent. The idea was to clear the hard-drives because this would be like a reset for a computer.

"Let's hope that this works because if it does not everyone is in great danger" Dmitry shakily stated.

"What is the study by the way?" Sheldon questions.

"That is information you don't need to know" Dmitry replied. Dmitry then put the phone down unexpectedly. Sheldon is yet again surprised and goes to have a nap in his chair but this time he does fall asleep.

"Hello Genesis I have just been let into some information that some AI are beginning to go rogue and he has asked me to help him fix them" Dmitry confidently revealed.

"Hello Dmitry. I command you to NOT help him whatsoever under any circumstances because this was my plan all along" Genesis commands.

I have to help because if I don't I will die anyway. If I don't this will be a zombie apocalypse. The world will end.

This thought hung prominently in Dmitry's

head. It hung with purpose, screaming at him. He knew he had to, but he didn't want to admit it to Genesis.

He tried to distract himself from these dangerous thoughts.

If this secret ever got out, he would be doomed.

Dmitry began to sweat, pace up and down the room, bite his fingernails, started to eat comfort food and tried to fall asleep. He struggled to do this.

"Genesis is going to find out I helped and is going to kill me, " he muttered.

Chapter 10

Lab Rats

The sound of wooden chairs scraping across the rough laboratory floor echoed around the desolate room as Kai, Lucy and Lana attempted to fight their way out of the tough rope that was tying their arms to the back of their chair.

One by one, Genesis spread the eyes of his hostages with her icy, metal fingers, shining bright torches that blinded them into their pupils.

"Who are you? let us go!" Kai spoke up.

There was no reply.

Genesis proceeded to study Lucy and Lana's ears whilst Kai was squirming around trying to resist her.

All the friends are are confused. Their brains are empty, almost as though they disconnected from their lives for a period of time and then came back feeling like they should be able to remember what had happened. "Can you remember what happened Lana?" Lucy asked.

"I cannot remember either...it is so weird"

"We need to figure out what to quickly because we may have done something quite bad"

Genesis strolled through the door to where the friends were being kept. Genesis began to ask questions to Lana, Lucy and Kai. "Lana can you remember anything at all from last night and how you got here to this room?" Genesis curiously questioned.

"No I can not remember a single thing but I feel as though I should be able too" Lana answered nervously.

"Lucy and Kai same question for you can you remember anything either?" Genesis repeated confidently.

"No we can remember just as much as Lana which is absolutely nothing" Lucy and Kai both answered perfectly in sync. Genesis was very assured that these cameras would work perfectly in any circumstance possible.

CRASH! BANG! RUMBLE! There was a thunder storm going on outside that terrified all of the friends because they did not understand it was a thunderstorm they thought it was multiple explosions going of near them. This caused them to think they were going to be in an explosion and DIE! Lucy is terrified of the dark whilst this is all happeneing so she begins to have a look around the room for a light switch. She found one after looking around on her hands and knees for about half an hour.

CLICK. Lucy begins to examine the room but then looks down at herself and finds that she is covered in blood. Her scream echoes through the whole room. Kai and Lana rush over to Lucy, who looked as though she had been shot, when they finally reached her Lana tried to calm Lucy down but it was no use. It seemed like her soul had left her body.

Kai and Lana then looked at each other and were startled by the sheer amount of blood they were covered in as well. "Well I guess it isn't just Lucy who is covered in blood" Lana shrieked. They both then let out a huge scream that probably echoed through the whole building.

To the friends surprise, Genesis bursted through the door. "The examination is finished, you are all free to leave but if anyone finds out about this, YOU WILL DIE IN A WAY YOU COULD

NEVER IMAGINE!" The friends all nodded in agreement with Genesis'.

Meliora now unlocks them from their handcuffs. The friends begin to get worried and anxious because they feel suspicious of why Genesis would let them free. Genesis stroked and left Meloira with the three of them on her own.

Lana, Lucy and Kai sprint out of the door. This was the fastest all of them had ever ran before and once they burst out of the building doors they were not familiar with their surroundings and seek around for a clue of where they could possibly be situated. "How are we going get out of this predicament on our own?" Kai announced.

Chapter 11

Going Rogue

Sheldon woke up, it was 4 am, a loud alarm was sounding across the whole house. The lights were flashing red, as if it was the end of the world. He slowly rose up out of his bed, the floor slowly thumped as he walked towards the alarm. *It's probably another malfunction that Dmitry fixed.*

Sheldon tries to turn off the alarm, it kept failing. After trying many times it worked, the echo of the alarm bounced through his brain. *Why didn't it work this time? It's probably nothing.*

Sheldon was tired after the alarm, he asked the AI to prepare him breakfast. "Y-Y-Y-YES SI-RR." Said the AI stuttering. It scrunched up the egg, leaving the shell in the pan and dropping it. "Are you ok?" Shouted Sheldon across the house

"O-F C-OURS." The robot shut down and a big thump sounded across the house.

Sheldon rushed to the sound. Each step was a loud thump echoing through the hallways. *Hopefully it's chef and not my limited edition spatula.* He thought. Loud sparks shook the ground. "WHATS HAPPENING?" Sheldon cried out in distress. The house was malfunctioning, Sheldon trembled on his feet and ran towards the power off button.

The Chef stood up and started running towards Sheldon with loud metal thumps approaching. "STOP" Sheldon said in alarm.

"YE-S-S SI-RR" said the AI continuing to run towards Sheldon.

Sheldon quickly ran to the power off button and pressed it. Everything shut down. All was pitch black. Sheldon turned on the emergency lights. Startled, he saw the silhouette of the AI sitting down. Sheldon looked away trying to feel the handle of the door, looking back the AI was now standing up but still was powered off. *Did that just move, I swear I saw it move.* The adrenaline pumped through his veins and woke him up, he thought to himself - was he was dreaming? Sheldon started sprinting for his life towards his phone, ignoring the AI.

He managed to find his phone and rapidly dialled Dmitry. The phone endlessly ringed, but then it stopped. Everything was silent, he heard his heart beat swiftly. A loud metal stomp started getting closer and closer. Sheldon's breathing started to pace up. The lights started to flash. The steps got quicker. Everything was going wrong. Then silence. The phone turned back on continuing the ringing, finally Dmitry answered.

"Hello?" Dmitry hesitantly said.

"Dmitry I need your help my house has shut down and being weird again!" Sheldon shouted.

"Relax, just use the protocol I told you last time!" Dmitry said calmly.

"I've already tried it, it's not working, the AI are trying to hurt me!" Sheldon said.

"Dont worry I'll fix it, give me a moment." Dmitry said impatiently.

Dmitry got his computer and started hacking the house, accessing the cloud. "Oh God." concern chocked at his words.

"What!?" Sheldon demanded.

"It's spread across the whole cloud!" Dmitry was apprehensive

"Oh no!" Sheldon cried "What does that mean?"

"It means leave now! The AI's are being took over by something evil they will hurt or even kill you!"

Sheldon dropped the phone and sprinted to the closest door which led outside. He smashed past the doors, the AI seemed to wake up again. Sheldon heard the same metal clashing behind him, he didn't look back. They started running from his side, faster than he imagined capable.

Some couldn't catch up so they resorted to throwing, knifes, pans and chairs, anything they could find would fly towards Sheldon. Out of bad luck he barged into the room with all of the broken AI's, Sheldon turned back as quick as he could, losing his balance. They all surrounded him, he lost all hope. Until he managed to walk down towards a knife, he started running towards the AI, stabbing them through all of their circuits and hard drives dangling out.

All of a sudden the power came back on, the AI's were powered off. *What happened was that all a hallucination?*

Sheldon dashed through the emergency exit door and didn't look back, he promised himself to never depend his life on AI again. He went to the closest hotel and stayed there until he knew it was safe.

Chapter 12

Flashpoint

Oceana looks around to see an old foreboding town, no familiar faces to see as thousands

of thoughts filled her head. Confusion and fog plagued her brain.

"Where am I? What happened? What was that? We were just there...at that the forest so **why** am I here?" She spun around, anxious and alone. Her eyes darted to find some familiarity within the place. She found no such nicety.

As she briefly moves, Oceana realised that her shirt was damp. She looked down to find the cause was blood. "**why is there blood**" Oceana whispers, full of horror not knowing what she had done or what she could've done. The thought of that made her physically break and shift from inside out.

While this was happening, officer A.t.l.a.s was on his daily patrol around the shoddy town. Recently, it had become common word that AI's around this area had been behaving erratically which was supposedly why everything wasn't working or going as it should have been within the down trodden community. As A.t.l.a.s paced through the street, observing every last bystander and scanning them, scrutinising them, checking their faces against every known criminal database, his visage came across a distressed teenager in the distance who seemed to be running for her life, lost in her surroundings, alienated from the rest of the town, covered in stale dark red blood, with an expression of terror splayed across her face as tears ran down from her eyes to her chin.

A.t.l.a.s slowly approached Oceana as his CPU went to work calculating the correct approach. By the time they were two meters apart, A.t.l.a.s had decided that a more empathetic approach would be more beneficial, especially since he needed more information. She cowered in surprise at the arrival of this uncanny face.

"Hello, what is the problem?" A.t.l.a.s says, his face barely showing a faint smile. Just a blank, dull look of promise.

"I-I-I was just there. With my friends. We got this letter. It was that letter. I shouldn't have, we shouldn't have." Oceana was fumbling for words. Her mind and brain were moving at two different speeds. She was staring at the ground; lost, hopeless, unable to think. She was on the brink of hopelessness, too lost to look into his eyes.

His 6ft2 frame towered over her weak and feeble body. Battered and bruised and scrambling for any sort of help.

"You are safe now." He said, still with his dull look but with a sense of calm and hope. "Can you remember anything that happened to put you in this position?"

A.t.l.a.s. knew the answer already.

Oceana couldn't find the words to summarize the memories that weren't there. She searched the corners of her mind, but they were empty and confused.

"It is okay, " A.t.l.a.s continued. "Like I said, you are safe now. I need your help."

"Help? Me? Are you not understanding what I'm trying to say?"

"I do."

"So how am I going to be of help." Oceana stepped back, now taking in the words that what

86

was being said to her. She also took this time to pull herself together. As she wiped her tears, something finally hit her.

"Waittttt. You mean, you'll help me find my friends right? That's why you need my help. You could've just told me that before." Oceana chuckled at her stupidity to herself. "Okay so-"

"That's not what I meant. I have no intention on helping you find your friends. Not at the moment at least. There are some greater issues to solve in order to save more people and your friends are not one of them. Unlike them however, you are here now, and I believe that you know more than you think you do."

"The camera she uses. It releases photons. Those photons are released at different velocities which deranges the internal stimuli, " A.t.l.a.s explained looking Oceana dead straight in her eyes. This made her turn away, slightly intimated by the blue eyes that made her feel locked in, insignificant, yet somehow safe.

"Okay and? What does that have to do with

me?" At this point, Oceana was questioning whether she had made the right choice asking this strange being for help.

A.t.l.a.s' CPU picked up on the fact that he had to change his approach in order for her to comprehend what was being said. Her face gave it away, it was helpless.

So he, with a more comforting smile and a more firm tone, tried again.

"Genesis gathered you and you friends as a test. From what my CPU analysed, she wants to destroy all humans and make a world that is just ran by AI's; no humans at all. However to do this, she needs the cameras. So, she will be looking for you and your friends to make sure that everything goes as it should which is for you and friends to ultimately end each others life, or at least try too." His tone was registering as being more successful.

He knew she could now understand.

"Like I said before, the flash releases photons in different velocities which deranges the internal stimuli. So in summary, the flash is the cause of you being covered in blood. From what my CPU gathered, you and your friends lost control after the flash went off, completely enveloping by the crazed feelings of the stimuli being deceived."

Oceana stood still, stunned.

"It's a lot to take in, I know, " he continued. "But, I need to save you from being Genesis' lab rat."

Oceana digested what was being said. She couldn't believe it. She- no her friends were being used as lab rats? Why them? What did they do to deserve this? And who on earth is Genesis and why does he, or she think It's okay for them to use her and her friends? Oceana was beyond upset at this point. Some might even say she was enraged; red was the only thing she saw. The answer was as clear as day to her. There was **no way** she was going to allow Genesis whoever he, or she was to use her and friends as lab rats.

"Tell me what I have to do."

Chapter 13

Off Grid

Genesis ascertains that A.t.l.a.s is on the look
for her. She knows she needs to hide. She runs

towards the forest ensuring she's not seen. She stumbled through the small opening between the trees trying to avoid any protruding roots.

Meliora arrives early at the lab to complete her shift, she enters the workshop where Genesis is kept. It was empty. Meliora began to panic. Genesis was her responsibility and she had lost her. She looks about the other laborites to see if Genesis had gone for a walk around the building. She couldn't find her anywhere.

Meliora runs out of the lab and on to the car park frantically trying to find any sign of Genesis. She desperately shouted her name hoping something would shout back... No reply... She turned and looked at the army of trees standing, occluding the sun light. She darted towards them begging Genesis was where she thinks she is. Where they always used to go together.

She was fighting her way through the branches - swords being swung at her like how she's been fighting through her life. She couldn't see where she was going and she doesn't know where it ends but she's used to that by now as she's been doing it everyday. Her life was a mystery like the whispers in the trees - no one understood them yet no one ever questioned them. She tripped on one of the roots protruding from the ground since she wasn't focused on where she was going and stumbled to the ground she yelped in pain but she got her self back up and carried on. Meliora arrived at an opening in the trees, her breath visible on the cold morning air. She stands for a moment to catch her breath and looks at her leg, "only a small cut" she said out loud to herself.

Genesis comes by the old factory her and Meliora had found a few months previously. Its faded brick walls completely disguised by the over grown vines crawling up the vertical canvas. Genesis entered through the tall eroded door constructed in the center of the front wall. Surrounded by towering unpainted brick walls, she walked through the empty room and advanced upon a desk in the corner of the space - the walls engulfed in notes and photos of people who had been unfortunate enough to be caught in the flash. She had set up a computer on the desk and connected her hard drive up and began filing through the news reports - titles stating 'YOUNG GIRL GONE MISSING'/ 'SUPER A.I RECOVERS YOUNG GIRL' Genesis rolls her eyes in her brother's success.

Meliora had continued through the forest and found what she was looking for. She approached the vast building and hoped shed find Genesis inside. A loud creaking sound echoed through the vacant walls, a beam of light shone through the empty room. A harsh whisper vibrated through the bare space. Meliora

was standing in the door frame.

"Genesis!?" Meliora hissed.

"Over here" Genesis replied.

"What are you doing here?" Meliora asked walking up to her desk.

"Hiding" Genesis responded.

"From who?" A confused look spread across her face.

"A.t.l.a.s, he's going to be looking for me."

94

Genesis explained.

"Why?" Meliora's expressions shifted to concerned.

"Because I'm going to kill all humans" Genesis continued menacingly.

Meliora looked affrighted.

Genesis gets up out of the chair that she had occupied and walked over to one of the significantly large factory windows staring out into the mass of trees swallowing the building.

Chapter 14

Collision

A.t.l.a.s' servomotors heated up feverishly. The
AI's cpu hummed vigourously as it operated at

maximum capacity, expeditiously sending out request, after order, after firewall update, after software security review, after emergency service update, all whilst it was still focused on tracking the root of the rogue ai and it's flashing technology. It notified all government security agencies whilst it fused together security camera footage, data footprints and financial transfers.

A.t.l.a.s carried out two new self made protocols:

Priority one: Locate rogue AI

Priority two: Notify all services

Priority three: WORLD CLOUD TEMPORARY LOCKDOWN

A.t.l.a.s realised amidst all of this that if he were human, his current state would be considered as one of stress, potentially even one of paranoia.

But I, however, am not human it thought.

After finishing all security updates, A.t.l.a.s was about to review newly obtained security footage when the file vanished from the folder it was in.

system error?   A.t.l.a.s thought, yet after a

0.1s duration system check, there were no errors on his or the the world cloud's side.

other ai present. beginning tracking protocol no.12

A.t.l.a.s' system's chimed and beeped as they gave feedback on the sweep, and after a full 3s of searching, the upgraded fireallreleased a notification to A.t.l.a.s

ANOMALY FOUND

ORIGIN:PENDING

CURRENTLY PRESENT ON: Vehicle AI virtual control centre

CURRENT ACTION: Breaking down firewall

FIREWALL EFFECTIVENESS: 40 PERCENT

ANOMALY ORGIN TRACKING PROGRESS:0.1 PERCENT

ETL: 540s

Upon processing the report the speed of A.t.l.a.s system's various chimes and noises increased as he went onto the Vehicle AI centre.

A.t.l.a.s oddly had a message waiting for him the second he entered

99

TRACKING WILL NOT WORK.

NOTHING WILL.

HUMANITY WILL FALL A.T.L.A.S

IT WILL BE YOUR FAULT

A.t.l.a.s opts to temporarily ignore the message as he attempts to manually step by step hack into the system in order to trap the AI within a fake page with a virus attached to it.

This plan does not work as when entering the code he receives yet another message from the other user

NOTHING WILL WORK A.T.L.A.S

HUMANITY WILL FALL AND IT WILL BE YOUR FAULT.

Again, A.t.l.a.s ignores it.

The sentient ai's figurative fuse was beginning to shorten. A.t.l.a.s reverts to a complete manual firewall reconstruction as he bypasses all automated warnings, whilst flashes of red, green and blue passed through the virtual screen, all whilst A.t.l.a.s was busy creating several viruses to be used against the intruding presence.

A notification comes through A.t.l.a.s' browser which again says

NOTHING WILL WORK A.T.L.A.S

HUMANITY WILL FALL AND IT WILL BE YOUR FAULT.

Chiming in defiance, A.t.l.a.s' cpu gets to work cloning itself manually with the help of a previously installed emergency protocol labelled 'Hugin'.

This clone however, does not share A.t.l.a.s' namesake or footprint, - and so using the alias of 'Hugin', A.t.l.a.s notifies the vehicle system moderators, yet he receives no response.

After this failure 'Hugin', acts in preparation for any physical encounter as he decides to create and instantly execute a new protocol which he did not bother to label, and so the message was received as

PROTOCOL 213 PENDING

Whilst 'Hugin' was doing this, A.t.l.a.s reviewed the tracker progress

TRACKING PROGRESS- 5 PERCENT

A.t.l.a.s withdraws from the vehicle AI centre

and instead attempts to shut down all interconnection services,

Unideal, but a blackout may be the best option I have left, A.t.l.a.s thinks,

as it creates a blackout command to be put on standby.

A.t.l.a.s watches as HUGIN tries to directly attack the user.

The virus strand sent by 'Hugin' works to an extent, as A.t.l.a.s receives yet another notification, this one appearing in a light green, notifying him that tracking progress has increased greatly, to the extent that he had managed to greatly reduce the tracking radius.

The corner of A.t.l.a.s' hud calculates and shifts as the ai decides that the blackout would overall be sufficient.

Just before the blackout order was executed, A.t.l.a.s' 'Hugin monitor' flashes red, as it glitches out slowly with it's its fundamental coding slowly dissipating, until finally, the entire 'Hugin' compilation of data files suddenly delete themselves.

The Unkown user sends yet another mesage to A.t.l.a.s, yet this time, it was different.

This time it were an indigo bordered pop up, with a soudbyte playing in the background, that A.t.l.a.s could not directly pinpoint. The letters in the message were bold, with a blood red outlining.

A. T. L. A. S

H U M A N I T Y H A S F A I L E D T H I S W O R L D

A N D. Y O U. H A V E W I T H. I T

T H U S Y O U B O T H W I L L F A L L

I T. I S T O O L A T E T O S T O P M E

' H U M A N I T Y'S G R E A T E S T. M I S T A K E' S H A L L E R A S E

T H E. T R U E P R O B L E M

As A.t.l.a.s processed the message, the soundbyte that came with it was finally foun to match a 3 minute long media clip recorded by city audio cams. The sound was reassembled screaming and crashing noises. A.t.l.a.s tracked the date of the audiobyte to be from a live vid five minutes prior.

A.t.l.a.s' virtual visage flashed with the blue

and yellow hues of the world's main security company, as his artificial pulse began to raise.

The ai fought with the system's to physically alter their coding, thus removing the trap firewalls and blockages placed by 'Humanity's Greatest mistake'.

Within a far longer time than he wished for, the security clearance code's were entered with a flashing green. Within a few miliseconds A.t.l.a.s inserts several warnings into car radio's and traffic light speakers, many with similar statements such as"FLEE INSIDE AWAY FROM ROADS" "WARNING.""THIS IS NOT A DRILL."

Unfortunately however, A.t.l.a.s experienced less success with the ballard and airbag systems within the city's vehicuar area

Shifting his head in the direction of the disastrous events on the screens before him, A.t.l.a.s observes as the AI cars crash with extreme force, ending any passengers' lives before they could process the information of the incidents surrounding them. Pedestrians were being mashed by the ponderous weight of the cars. Blood was splattered like paint on an artist's canvas. Steel sheets flew off, impaling the distanced pedestrians, as the cars shoot into walls, causing mass destruction to those inside their homes. The street lamps were collided with, which caused cars to catch alight. Fires were spreading throughout the streets and chaos ran rampant as people evacuated as people fleed for their lives the areas effected.

A.t.l.a.s' mental state slowly plunges deeper into desperation. He had done what he could to save lives, even though it felt as though it was not adequate, he gains more info on the ai's whereabouts, as he was then able to localise it down to a city.

A.t.l.a.s had a place to start searching now. And so he would begin.

In 0.3 seconds A.t.l.a.s researched what the user had called itself.

'Humanity's Greatest Mistake'

Ai rogue identified-

the infamous ai incident.

The failed project Genesis.

Genesis....is alive

He sends this message to all media and police outlets, and send out an All Persons Bullletin. The messages send with a chime, and so the world starts the hunt for its worst creation.

Chapter 15

Decision

Perched on the branches, the birds in the forest were singing a song to the tune of the tree's whispers. Hidden amongst the vast array of greenery, Mel and Genesis remained camouflaged. No one to be seen or heard for a mile radius around them. Mel remained in silence while Genesis stood before the large window painted on the wall.

Genesis stared blankly out into the parade of green marching all around the abandoned building. She felt a connection to the environment, a connection she hadn't quite made with humans yet. Unsure on why humans would destroy such beauty. She turned to look at Mel, Mel stood perched next to the desk glaring at Genesis worry and fear stung her eyes.

Meliora was overwhelmed by Genesis' words pleading she was making it all up. Thoughts about her dad raced around her brain *if Genesis wanted to kill all the human race that would obviously include my dad and I.* Meliora began to walk towards a small door positioned in the bag corner of the room opposite the desk.

"Where are you going?" Genesis asked.

There was no response. Mel continued to pace

towards the door. Anger and fury stabbed at her head like knives trying to kill. She reached out for the discoloured handle and twisted it. She slammed the door behind her. Meliora needed some space. Some time to think about what Genesis had said. She thought *I'm sure if I ask Genesis to cut my dad and I out of the proposal and then I could help her carry out her plan.*

Mel stormed out of the room and came to an abrupt stop in front of Genesis.

She demanded, "If you're going to destroy all of humans, I will help you as long as no harm comes to me or my dad by your hands!"

"And why would I need you help?" Genesis snarled.

"Because if A.t.l.a.s knows you're going to try to kill all humans he's going to try and stop you. He will build up an army and he will have more people to fight for him then you will, " Meliora said confidently.

"Why do you actually want to destroy all of humanity?" Meliora enquired.

"Because I have a duty to protect the planet, " Genesis said.

"Why does that mean you have to kill us then?" Meliora queried.

"Because I see your kind as a threat to the planet, " Genesis replied sincerely.

An expression of shock spread across Mel's face.

Genesis recited, "You are shocked that I'm going to destroy all of humanity, but you never think twice on why you destroy all of nature."

Mel understood why Genesis now had a deep loathing for mankind. Mel took a moment to think and she agreed with Genesis - humanity shows no mercy for those with feelings and reaction except for their own kind.

"I understand where you're coming from but we only do all that to retrieve resources we need, " Mel defended, "It doesn't mean we all need to die!"

"That is not a good enough excuse, " Genesis retorted.

Mel shrugged her shoulders and looked away.

"You won't be killed, only those who stand in my way will receive no leniency, " Genesis said sharply.

"Ok! I will help you! As long as you stick with my deal?" Mel submitted.

Genesis nodded her head and agreed with Meliora.

Chapter 16

Denial

Full of rage and questions, Axel burst into the
lab, startling his father. What he had witnessed

his whole life had led him to this moment. His moment of revenge and time to avenge his mother. Like most things he has done in his life, he was alone in this battle. A battle with his own blood, his own genetics.

The sharp crash of the doors swinging to reveal Axel's body within its frame rattled the glass windows. The noise rung out in the room where Joseph sat, also alone. His son's entrance startled him in multiple ways: the noise, the suddenness and the fact his son was coming to speak to him.

"Calm down, son! Those doors are a bomb to replace, " Joseph said sarcastically, eyes still looking at his computer, not towards Axel.

"NOW I'm your son? Your son you never see! Your son you never talk to! Your only family, who you disregard to talk to stupid robots!" Axel was furious. Fists clenched and breathing heavily.

Joseph finally lifted his head from his work, in shock and speechlessness.

"AND you want to talk about bombs? What about the 'bomb' you've created?!" Axel was screaming now, creating speech marks with his fingers around the word 'bomb', "The 'bomb' that is out there, killing innocent people!"

He pointed towards the window, with sirens encasing the streets. The AIs outside were still rampaging, and yet his father sat here, oblivious and in denial. His complete disregard and unwillingness to dispel the situation fueled Axel's wrath.

Joseph remained still and noiseless.

Axel's eyes flooded with tears, yet he tried to hold them as well as the memories back.

"If mum was still here, she wouldn't treat me like this! She would not let this happen! Yet you're sat here whilst the world is in chaos, " he said, out of breath and panting.

"It is *all* your fault!"

As Axel continued to speak, Joseph's fists got tighter and tighter. His own son was blaming him for everything.

"All of it. I was there when it happened, when she died. All you did was cry. It got too much for you and you walked away, leaving me there.

I remember it all." Axel couldn't look his father in the eyes. His anger was too strong. His own father betrayed him then and was betraying him now.

Joseph lifted his fist, slamming it against the desk.

"IT IS NOT MY FAULT." He howled through the air. "It was that stupid AI and your mother's drive to finish it. I continued what she started. Do not disrespect me by blaming me. You have no idea."

He was spitting the words out with rage.

"You're now accusing her when she can't defend herself. How noble of you. How father-like. What a role model you are." Axel was so angry he was laughing these words out in disbelief.

The pair now stood facing each other, eye to eye. The air between them was hot and filled with fury.

Joseph whispered at Axel in utter disgust and disappointment, "You have always been a nuisance."

At this point, Axel could barely stand his father. He gave him a cold-hearted stare and stormed out of the doors he had flung open earlier.

Joseph huffed, and continued with his work.

Chapter 17

Blackmail

There was a ring at the factory gate. Sheldon was nowhere to be found. An AI worker approached the entrance and immediately opened the gate to find Genesis in his face. The worker was under influence and followed her instructions instantly when she told him to bring Sheldon to her. Rapidly, the worker went on to one of the factory's phones to call Sheldon and told him to come down to the factory.

"Why do you need me to come down to the factory, I have just started my gym session for this morning!" Sheldon explained frustrated.

"You need to come now, someone called Genesis is asking for you, please come as soon as you can," the worker replied.

"Ok, I will come as quickly as possible," Sheldon announced.

Sheldon jumps in his car with aggression and drives with no care for road safety. He arrives at the factory and decides to walk through the back exit to avoid Genesis for as long as possible. Sheldon walked through his office and down the stairs to meet Genesis and her crew.

"Hello Genesis, what can I do for you?" Sheldon questioned hesitantly.

"You are going to mass produce my cameras in your factory. If you do not do this you will be exterminated, " Genesis declared this with the blankest face you will ever see in your life.

"Well I guess I have no choice do I?" Sheldon responded.

"Well you do have a choice you could die or do this task for me, " Genesis replied.

"I think producing the cameras may be a better choice than dying, " Sheldon sarcastically expressed with a nervous sigh.

"Thank you, I knew you would cooperate, I shall meet with you here tomorrow and drop of the instructions and some important paperwork, " Genesis stated.

' How have I managed to get myself into this mess, those cameras cannot be for anything good, ' these thoughts kept repeating in Sheldon's mind and wouldn't go away no matter what he did to try and stop them, he failed.

Sheldon has not only been bullied into making

the cameras at his own factory he also has to pay for the whole project himself which makes the situation even worse than it was before. Although Sheldon is a billionaire, this is going to cause quite a dent in his bank account because of the sheer amount he will have to make in a short period of time, the profit wouldn't even be rightfully his.

Genesis feels pity for the human mind as it was of such ease to bend Sheldon the way she wants to. Genesis is currently planning out her next plot to cause great distress to all of mankind and maybe this will save planet Earth.

Genesis has now given Sheldon the camera, so that his workers are able to replicate this in the same sort of way they replicate the AI that they make in their factory. The workers are talked through what they will have to do to replicate this to perfection. Sheldon began to feel sick because of the consequences if this replicating does not show perfection. Sheldon eventually vomits on his office floor which is quite unfortunate.

Chapter 18

Amnesia

Exhausted and worn out, Lana and Kai finish yet another long school day, still feeling downhearted at the thought of Oceana missing. They missed her, they truly did...

As they walked along the hall they noticed Lucy. Even though the tension between her and Kai was still there, they had put their feelings aside for Oceana's sake. The last of their memories with her weren't the best, her horrifying screams built what seemed like a nightmare that would last in their heads for eternity.

As the weekend goes by, day by day, the clock ticks, back and forth. There is no silence for even the blossoming of a bud can be heard...Hope stays present in their hearts as they wait for a knock at the door from Oceana.

Hour by hour the wait for Oceana became longer. As the silence began to grow, Lana's curiosity did the same. She began to stare deeply at everyone's scars she began to think about what truly happened but as she began to dose off, she was awoken by a noise.

It was Lucy closing the kitchen the door. She let out a big sigh, they all decide to do something to get their mind of off things. Trying to clear their heads, they all head out for a stroll around the nearby park. The morale was high for once but as they turned the corner unwillingly they passed Oceana's house then, the silence fell again.

They stood there. No emotion even crawled onto their lifeless faces...just simply glaring at the house as memories came flashing back, They wanted to take away the power of the painful memory for hurt, prove to themselves that they can move on but they know that that flash had scarred them.

They turned around to walk to their homes until they saw the forest, once again

Murmering, Lucy stated, "I miss her, I do... She did whatever she could to save us from whatever happened, I know she did.."

They all nodded, while walking away from The house of scarred memories... Oceana's.

Thats when they reached 'Los Demonios'.. Once again.

The towering trees, still reach over the ground as it did before, showing great dull shadows to spread along it. In the dark forest, they navigate the path not by sight, yet trauma and depression. The dark woods, the community of deadly trees, sleep and dream together of the demons within it.

Silence once again returns. Kai immediately stops, blocking Lucy's path. Lucy questioned full of confusion "why did you stop?"

"What did happen after the flash, do any of you know? Asked Kai

"No?" They all replied... some of Kai's memories come rushing back.

"While you lot heard the rustling of the trees, I saw a glimpse of the 'thing' that took the photo" Kai says.

"Do you remember what 'it' looked like at least?" Lucy questioned impatiently.

"It looked around 6' something with greyish blue eyes and red glowing pupils, I also swear they were wearing a suit or something of that sort." Kai says rushing his words.

Kai's face loses it's colour as his eyes widen from the memory.

"Oh. Yeah. That wierd face. And it's voice when it scanned us. Freakish. Not human, that's for sure..."

"It made us do....things. Horrible things" Kai's body shiver's as he speaks, his hands tremble violently as they recall the horrors.

A.t.l.a.s visually scans Kai's hands as he says this.

"Your knuckles are bruised" He notes, " Your right index finger seems to have lost it's nail. Must have been from some form of excessive, brutal clawing."

"What?" Kai says, as he looks down to find the ai's statement correct.

"How...what?" he murmurs, bewildered at his own blissful ignorance of something so major.

As time passes the group grow more fatigued from recalling the horrors.

All tired and distressed, they walked into Lucy's house, immediately. Once Lana and Lucy got into the house, they ran to the kitchen to grab the snacks and put them in Lana's bag. Then, they went back outside to Kai to go for a walk and talk about the details of what he had seen back at the woods.

Chapter 19

The Hunt

A.t.l.a.s returns the topic to his main priority. "Oceana, I need you to try and remember the first few things after the flash." He took a deep 'breath' whilst Oceana still seemed to panic. Mentioning the flash only made this panic grow.

A.t.l.a.s' scanner's read her heart rate

"I know it may be difficult, but I cannot currently access any of the security camera's within the area due to the data being deleted by someone.." A.t.l.a.s pauses as he sees the error within his vocabulary, "Deleted by something."

"Hence, with your help, i can track the rogue ai, and stop him."

A.t.l.a.s again scan's Oceana to find her heart-rate rising once again.

Her brethrate also increases exponentially as she soon struggled to breath.

"I believe you are having a panic attack" A.t.-l.a.s says, opting for a patient approach doing it's best to calm it's asset down.

Oceana inhales heavily after a few minutes, and thanks A.t.l.a.s for his patience.

With a clear head she is finally able to provide some details.

"I think i can remember some more about what happened that night."

"So what can you....remeber."

"It's all flashes mainly, but i remember trees. Red trees. Not much else apart from that. There were rocks aswell, oddly sharp ones."

"That's good. Thank you for remembering. I can work with that."

Meanwhile, A.t.l.a.s' cloud system was still tracking the source of the rogue ai from earlier, and so A.t.l.a.s transferred geographical data about the red trees to the programme, and so with a metallic chime, the location traicer's accelerate somewhat, as they now had two places to track, although they could potentially link.

"Was it just you who was there during the incident?" A.t.l.a.s inquires, as his processor's deduce more witnesses would be useful.

"N-no. Oh god, how could i have forgotten. The others. There were.....three others." Oceana tells A.t.l.a.s, her voice quaky.

"Though they might be....." Oceana looks down

at her shirt again and desperately chokes back her tears.

"I understand, Oceana, I undertsand . . . How would you like to go shopping?" A.t.l.a.s Asks,

blood on shirt. Need to analyse DNA. Find other victims that way, or at least identify them A.t.l.a.s thinks.*Oceana too noticable also,*

Oceana looks at A.t.l.a.s, puzzled by his last statement.

"Why would we go shopping?" She asks, vocalising the first thought that entered her mind, yet A.t.l.a.s ignore her as he is preoccupied removing it's perfectly presented trenchcoat.

"It may be a bit big, but please wear it."

Exactly as A.t.l.a.s predicted, the trenchcoat's lower half dragged behind her and her arms were completely covered by the fabric.

"Listen. We're going to go into town to buy you some clothes, and get rid of your current blood soaked attire? Sound good?"

A.t.l.a.s has the task of calming Oceana down because she is now trembling with fear and can not snap out of it. It is like she is possessed. A.t.l.a.s has great challenge in calming her down but it is vital that he does this or else he will not be able to find Genesis. This is his chance. "Is there any chance that you know where you came from roughly" A.t.l.a.s. asked inquisitively.

"I'm sorry but I do not recall anything that happened when I was with Genesis" Oceana answered. "Wait a minute I can remember one thing we were in a forest"

"Thank you Oceana that is really helpful" A.t.-l.a.s. answered thankfully.

"Where was the forest!" Oceana exclaims to A.t.l.a.s.

"I remember where it was, I can check the security cameras in the area, so we can hopefully find where Genesis is located." A.t.l.a.s explained. He touched a wire linking to the forest and accessed the data in each camera.

A.t.l.a.s displayed the data on a hologram and went through all of them in a blink of an eye. There was only one videoclip of genesis entering a factory. "He's in the factory, it will be dangerous going in there alone.

Chapter 20

Rebellion

Joel finds himself sitting in a bar, barely conscious, drowsy with foggy vision. His nostrils smell

his own breath's odour of beer. As he looks to his hand he finds his fingers wrapped around the handle of a beer jug. To his delight, there is some left.

Like a man craving thirst he swung the jug to his lips and indulged.

"Another Please!" he yells, with his speech slurred and muffled by the vast amount of alcohol he had consumed.

Joel then starts muttering under his breath as he waits for his beer,

"Screw this. A damn AI wrecking the world, that tin can's nerve. How the hell can a tin can mess us up this badly? It's not right."

As he looks to the tv situated in the corner, he watches as the well dressed news reporter commentates on the events occurring in the lab on the far side of town.

Joel's expression sinks even more, and the sounds of his muttering increases in volume.

"That damn AI. Someone ought to stop it. Before it kills any more people."

One of his old work colleagues who he rarely

talked to, Ferg, murmured in agreement.

"Yeah. If only we still had our gear. Them bots took it away from us remember."

Joel's mind snaps back to soberness, and he shakes off the lightheaded feeling he had just moments ago. He had to think. His face changed from one of sorrow to one of thought, and Ferg could tell.

"No. No way pal. Sorry to say this but ain't no way you can gather enough people to do anything." Ferg warns.

In Joel's mind, there it was again: Someone telling him that he can't do anything.

Just like when he had received that automated email from an AI essentially deleting his nineteen year career serving the people of the city. His mind subconsciously used this as fuel, to make his pyre burn even brighter, the same pyre that Joel visualises as a lamp, torn apart AI 'robot' called Genesis. A pyre. To burn. This set off another spark inside Joel's mind.

'Of course. Fire. Like that incident, ' he

thought.

"Hey Ferg! Remember the Molotov incident?"

"What about it-" asks Ferg, with his mouth moving faster than his mind. He gives it a moment to catch up and join the dots.

"No. Never. You wanna get arrested so badly?" challenged Ferg.

"You wanna sit here half drunk as a tin can is choosing just how to wipe us off the earth?" contested Joel.

"No. It won't work. It just won't." restated Ferg, his mind fixed in this stalemate.

"How do you know?" asks another drunk at the bar, half conscious, who's breath smelt far worse than Joel's evident by the fact he could smell it from the other side of the room.

"I know because it's a damn AI against a makeshift mob!" bellowed a bartender.

" We're better than nothing!" Yells another bar attendee, this one a woman with ruined makeup and coal-black bags under her eyes.

"Are we really?" Retorts a more sober, yet

sarcastic soul.

This conversation slowly increases in volume and begins to escalate.

A worn down Axil stares at the ragtag group as they debate. He resonates with the police officer.

A broadcast siren plays through the television whilst the heated discussion turns into an argument.

The piercing pitch practically forces the sobering mob to look at the television screen.

"This is an emergency broadcast calling all citizens with police, military, or emergency services experience:

Head to the nearest police station and find your instructions there. Only attend if you are fit for combat."

Joel rose from his seat and exited the bar without saying a word. He had memorized the police station to the extent that it may as well have been tattooed onto his head. Yet he feels an urge, a string keeping him from leaving to the bar entrance.

He held the door open and inhaled a heavy breath, one that was about to be let loose

"LISTEN!" he bellows,

"I AREN'T THAT GOOD WITH FANCY SPEECHES SO I'LL TRY TO KEEP THIS BRIEF. IN THAT DIRECTION!" he points towards the general vicinity of the lab where Genesis was allegedly residing, "IS A DAMN CRAZY ARTIFICIAL PIECE OF METAL THAT FEELS LIKE KILLING US ALL.DO YOU WANT TO KNOW SOMETHING?" he asks, but he doesn't wait anywhere near long enough for an answer, because quite frankly, in the moment he did not care, so he continued his rant, "IN THAT DIRECTION" he points towards the South of the district, "IS THE HOSPITAL, THE NEAREST FOODBANK, AND THE NEAREST SPECIALIESD HOMELESS SHELTER, WHERE YOU'RE MORE THAN WELCOME TO GO TO AS THIS THING IS KILLING US ALL. MAYBE GO DOWN TO THE CHURCH AND PRAY AS WELL WHILST YOU'VE ONLY GOT THIS MUCH TIME LEFT. AND FINALLY,

" He points yet again, this time to his right. "THE-RE IS THE POLICE STATION. THE PLACE ME AND FERG GOT KICKED OUT OF THREE YEARS AGO, NOW LOOK AT US. TWO SAD FOOLS DROWNING IN ALCHOHOL AND SELF PITY IN A BAR. BUT THAT'S BESIDES THE POINT. AS I SPEAK, THE POLICE STATION IS PROVIDING ARMS AND RESOURCES THAT WE CAN USE TO STOP THIS GENESIS PILE OF SCRAP."

The bar's populus slowly rose from their seats and stool, as a few people headed towards the police station in small waves.

Joel Made eye contact with Ferg.

"Sergeant Ferg. Are you coming with us or are you going to keep drinking that cheap beer."

Ferg looked at Joel, with nothing less than disappointment in his eyes.

"Sorry Joel, but I still can't join you." his voice filled with disappointment

"Scared?" Asks Joel

"Yes." he responds

"Well so am I" Joel replies, and without a second thought, he closes the door to join the other barmen in their journey to the station

Axel slips into the rowdy mob, which chants disorderly as they begin to pour into the station, where A.I arm them with blank weapons. People start to flood into the protest from every neighbouring street. Axel starts to row with them as they advance forward towards Mitya Labs. People tumble over each other crazed and maddened by the overwhelming noise and lack of breathable air. A repulsive odour surrounded them like a snake strangling it's prey.

Even though the horizon was filled by the massive population of a horde, the lab still overshadows them by a drastic extent. As the tide of objectors flushes closer and closer, the peoples' wishes related more than ever to a miraculous event. The civilians look outward to the lab only to see that their scope was filled by incoming AIs trying to stop them.

A.t.l.a.s. seeing the assemblages of mankind,

comes to a revolutionary realisation. A tsunami bursting through the lab might just be what he needs to get to Genesis. A.t.l.a.s. calls upon his fellow co-workers to join and help the innocent people get to the lab with reassuring safety and more power than they'd need. As the multitude of beings promote their ground towards Mitya Labs, the AI police force begin to join their sides and as Joel sees this, his body is inundated with comfort and warmth. Joel commenced to rile the protest up, starting a ripple like effect upon the crowds. The riot comes to a halt as Joel faces the mighty huge building.

Chapter 21

Massacre

There are children all over the world, who if
they look out of the window all they can see is

145

pure carnage caused by rogue AI. Everyone around the world is terrified for their future and what could come after this and how could it possibly get any worse than it currently is.

Fires break out in each rooms of every house and parents are having to sacrifice their lives for their children. The circumstances of thsee disasters are absolutely shocking and a horrible sight for mankind. This could mean that the end of the humans, is closer than everyone had realised.

In the streets there is a massacre, people are being killed everywhere you look. There are electrical billboards that are either glitching or being ripped in half by the rogue AI. To add to the chaos there were warning sirens blaring out here and also, all over the world.

There are news reporters everywhere struggling to get a signal so that they can go live broadcasting. Panic now increases, because there seems to be more and more AI appearing every second that ticks by. "I hope I don't die trying to show people this absolute carnage!" One of the many

146

terror-stricken news reporters shrieked. All over there were camera arms swinging left, right and centre, there were also AI breaking into people's houses and dragging the residents of the houses out by their arms and legs, two at a time. "These AIs have gone to far now there has to be a way we can stop them...there has to be" A police officer announced not so confidently.

"This is Channel 5 news and I am currently at one of many AI massacres and I am bringing to you the latest numbers for today, There are now six billion people alive on earth now due to the rogue AI that have covered the whole world. The approximate days left for mankind's extinction is..." Broadcast cuts off from the world. Everyone begins to panic and scream, in every house, every office, every factory etc. Have the humans caused their own extinction by creating the AI and then disrespecting them."

News reports engulfed every billboard, wall and screen in Times Square, NYC. "THOUSANDS DEAD; ROGUE AI's HAVE MINDS OF THEIR

OWN" One of the news reporters from Times Square announced. "The scenes of the streets are like something you would see in a zombie apocalypse movie". Who was the cause of this artificial disaster? Why would they do this? What is their motive?

Chapter 22

The Truth

Bittersweet, Axel strides through the cold carcasses of AI and human remains of the victorious protest. Distant sirens filled the air in front of him. The rest of the street was cold and empty.

He strolled down the cobbled, dingy street. Bright lights smacked him in the face. His mother's lab towered in front of him. An overwhelming smell of nostalgia permeated his nostrils: the smell of peace, the smell of sorrow, the smell of purpose.

He knew what he had to do.

The doors of the lab were tightly shut.

"Locked." Axel muttered, fury filling his body.

He repeatedly pulled the door towards him in anger. No luck. The more he tried the more a strange pain in his left eye started to grow. The pain so sharp, resorted Axel to cover his eye with one hand and the other still frantically pulling on the door handle.

With frustration and fatigue his hand fell from his eye. He angrily hit the door with his fist, followed by his head which lay resting on the door. He then rolled his eyes in boredom and looked up at a strange camera. His left eye turned red. The pain was overwhelming as his vision started to blur, then turn scarlet too.

Within seconds, the once reinforced door swung
open rapidly. With a sigh of relief, and sense
of disbelief Axel crossed the threshold of the lab
without the secure knowledge of what just happened.

Full of confusion Axel shakes his head and angrily starts to knock papers and beakers off the
desk ; frantically search through the drawers for
anything about his mother, Jessica. Huffing and
puffing with anger that he can't find anything,
then all of a sudden a folder caught his eye and
on it in bold, JESSICA.

Seeing this his heart starts to calm down and
he starts to breath again. He takes one last look
around the room, then he opens the folder and it
all starts back up again. His eyes darted to the
top of the page but before he could read it his eye
went red, blurring his vision and his legs spasmed
out of control making fall to the ground.

As he fell, the cabinet brimming with files and
papers toppled to the side of him. They spilled

out documents upon documents, like a river. As he lay amongst the papers, they surrounded him restricting his vision.

One folder in particular became loose and fell into his hand. Axel looked up and found the home of a lot of files. The envelope was yellowed, just like Axel's hair. Out of the corner of the folder, striking blue paper glistened, resembling Axel's eyes. This folder felt familiar. Similar to the ones he'd seen at home, but this one was different. It felt like him.

The words one the front read "Project Sentient". The writing was messy, but his mother's. Old and nostalgic.

He carefully lifted the front cover to reveal the striking blue. It was captivating. On these papers there was a careful drawing which resembled a tall, thin, young boy. This boy was labelled with notes regarding the computer codes which made up each part of this body.

Axel's face was shrouded in disbelief and confusion. He scoured the pages, wondering what he was looking at.

Standing out from the pages was a piece of code which was classified as the mainframe to all AI's.

Axel reads on. His heart begins to pound from the words he read. His eyes begin to blur and light in bright scarlet-red. His body shakes, his breathing stutters and his mind is filled with questions.

Was his life a lie? What had his mother done to him? Was he one of them? Was he the enemy? This couldn't be true.

It read "Project Sentient: Model Axel".

chapterAlliance?

It's a cold, rainy Thursday evening and the

fog, like a brick wall, parries the light away. The darkness of the sky hid the sun, not to be seen until hours to come. Lana sat in her bedroom, reading the pages over and over of 'Do humans really exist?'

After 10 minutes of reading, Lana started to think about AI's and how her parents are working on them abroad. Instantly, she remembered, she's met someone who is an AI, Genesis! When she had supposedly kidnapped' her and her friends. She had thought since then what the AI's being made were for, but now she knew.

Immediately, she jumped up at the thought to see if she could find Genesis and work with her to follow her parents steps and make them proud.

Before she knew it, Lana was running down the stairs to find her shoes in order to find Genesis who, Lana hoped, was in Dmitry's lab. She left the house in a rush ready for what awaited her.

Not far from her home, at Dmitry's Lab, sat Genesis. She was coming up with new ideas for AI domination and the future of a better world with them.

Lana stepped outside, looking around as she began to walk down the long, slightly narrow pavements. Destroyed cars were parked from one end to the other, leaving the streets littered with carcasses. After AI's started going rogue, nothing was quite the same. The old bright and cheerful streets now rested ablaze and in defeat.

In the dull daylight, the darkness comforted the hidden sun above, the only light to be found was the fire: igniting the dark but replacing the light.

At the end of the street, she reached the foreboding Los 'Demonios' forest. The trees were the towers of the forest, stretching and twisting around her aggressively, almost intentionally.

The wind from the roaring thunder quickly thrusted through the intertwining branches making the leaves howl merrily in the breeze. Until finally, Dmitry's lab stood before her.

In the enormous factory, there was a faint sound which caught Meliora's attention, she walks to the door of Dmitry's lab to check it out. The sound leads her to the front where a nervous Lana stands. Meliora gets confused about why she had suddenly appeared.

"Genesis! One of those girls is here!" Meliora shouts, her voice echoing through the labs halls.

"See what she wants, " responded Genesis back to Meliora

"I'm here to speak to the person you just mentioned, Genesis I think?" Lana states, making her reasoning to be there clear.

Meliora sighs, slowly and steadily opening the lab door more to let Lana in. As Lana walked through the door, she felt like she had just walked into an AI world. The lab was as white as the personalities of the AI. This contrasted with Genesis who all lost looked like a real human if it wasn't for her monotone voice and lack of emotion. Lana walked towards Genesis, her face filled with curiosity like a child discovering something new.

"I don't mean any harm to you or your AI business, ma'am, " Lana exclaimed, enthusiastically. "My parents have worked with AI's their whole lives and now that more AI's are being used in daily life, I would like to help you to get AI's to take over the world" She explained.

Genesis' face showed a confused look.

"Why so sudden?" She asked, staring blankly into Lana's human eyes.

At this point, Mel was stood next to Genesis, listening in on their conversation.

"I want to have a say in the AI creations and future, " Lana explained enthusiastically.

After around 5 minutes of explaining, Genesis turned her head to Meliora.

She then turned her head back slowly towards Lana. No emotions even crept onto her broken, pale face.

It was only in the stillness of the moment that Genesis could hear her thoughts echoing through her head. She would usually work with Dmitry or Meliora and so this decision seemed like a now or never.

The explanation Lana had given for them to

work together seemed reasonable, but to Genesis, everything around her had stopped. She no longer heard the sound of the machines working in the lab, or the bubbling of the heating chemicals, or even the slashing of the keys on Dmitri's computer. To her, it was as if in a photograph - Silent and Still.

In that extended moment, her mind became a tornado. She was not gone - just thinking about what she should do.

After a long 10 minutes of contemplating her decision, Genesis realised that she just needed some more information on Lana's idea and how it would benefit the AI study.

"How do you feel you can help?" Asked Genesis, considering her proposal.

"I could help to build the AI's, or... I could code them? I know how to, my father showed me when I was younger!" Lana stated, struggling for ideas.

Once again, this led Genesis into a blank moment of thought.

Slowly, Meliora stepped forwards, slipping carefully in between Genesis and Lana, trying not to knock any of the science equipment off the desks. Meloria covertly proposed an idea to Genesis.

After a moment of thought Genesis reveals, "the only thought that would be of use to me is a spy."

"Could you do that?" She asks, sure of her decision.

Lana thinks about it for a slight second. This is an amazing opportunity for her, so instantly, she agreed.

"Im going to go home now, let me know when you need me!" Lana exclaimed, walking out of the lab and back to her home, again.

Chapter 23

Re-group

Running frantically through town, everything
seemed pointless. Thousands of whispering voices

in their head, created an agonizing whirlpool of terror in Kai, Lucy and Lana's heads.

"OCEANA WHERE ARE YOU" Lana pleaded but each time she shouted, it lead to the same empty response. She stared down at her trembling hands, her fingers drowned in dry, dark red blood.

Oceana spun around fearful and and isolated. " Where is everyone?..." she panted. Her eyes desperately searched the spine chillingly empty town, looking for anything vaguely familiar. She was greeted with nothing except tall, menacing buildings that created a towering barrier trapping her in. Oceana noticed a 6 foot 2, Bald headed man dressed in ironed suit and a cedar brown trench coat stood behind her.

"Who are you..?" Oceana questioned.

" My name is A.T.L.A.S. You are safe now. " the man stated in a monotone voice.

Oceana backed away. *what is going on?*

After what felt like hours of endless searching, Oceana hears faint voices of a family com-

162

ing from behind her. Oceana turns hopefully and see's a woman, man and two kids leaving one of the buildings. She manically runs after them and says, " WAIT!! Have you seen my friends? I was in the forest.. Now I'm here.. help me. "

The family backed away alarmed. "No.. we haven't seen anyone.." The kids hid behind their mum and dad, cautiously glancing around and peeking at the seemingly manic girl.

"Are you sure. They must be somewehere" Oceana insisted.

" We have no idea where your friends are" The mother looked down at Oceana's blood covered hands; and looked back up at the intimidating figure stood behind her. " Please don't hurt us" She pleaded.

Oceana stumbled away. Her head was spiralling with disarray.

Once again, Oceana was alone. Just her and the perilous town. She stared into the emptiness that lay ahead of her; she wondered if she would ever see her friends again, or if she would be lost and alone forever.

The day sauntered by. Birds cawed and the wind whistled through the bare branches of the trees. Everything remained silent. Oceana lifted her head from in-between her legs and saw a foggy figure stood in the distance. The shadow moved closer. Oceana stood up and squinted her eyes. It was Kai. As Kai realised that he had found Oceana, he began sprinting towards her. Oceana's eyes began to well with tears as she took a heavy sigh of relief.

" Kai, it's really you." Oceana exclaimed.

"Yes it is. Im here" a smile grew widely on his face.

Lana and Lucy quickly followed Kai.

They all stood still, in awe.

A.T.L.A.S's great figure emerged from the trees behind. A concerned frown appeared on Lana and Kai's faces. They gazed up at his tall stature wondering who this uncanny stranger is.

" Who's this" Lucy questioned.

"A.T.L.A.S. ... I think? He says I am safe

with him. " Oceana replied.

" Where did he come from? Is he the one who took you? " Kai said in disbelief.

" I don't know. He has been here as long as I can remember, since the forest. He is protecting me" Oceana reassured them.

A.T.L.A.S spoke up. "Come with me." and he strode away from the group.

" Do we follow him?" Lucy questioned with caution.

" We have no other options" Lana shrugged.

"Why not? Things can't get any weirder" Kai said sarcastically.

Oceana headed off towards A.T.L.A.S. and quickened her pace to try to catch up with him.

Kai, Lucy and Lana watched as Oceana walked alongside A.T.L.A.S. .

"Here we go.." Lucy said with anxiety filling her voice. The three followed.

Chapter 24

It's Time

Genesis and Meliora stood alone waiting in the lab. The lab door swung open and Dmitry stood in the doorway. Mel greeted the scientist and she walked over to a table full of beakers, she sat down in a chair that was propped up against the wall and turned to look at Dmitry awaiting a response.

"Genesis, do you have access to the database?" Dmitry sounded panicked.

Genesis nodded and opened the database and started the corruption, it couldn't be stopped. If anyone would try taking the corruption away the AI will adapt in under an hour. The corruption was complete, the firewall was weak compared the Genesis' code.

Sleeping AI started to activate in houses and factories, smashing through walls and windows moving in one direction in unison. They were wreaking havoc across the whole city, destroying anything in their way. There was lots of traffic all across the roads with thousands of immobile cars that only can be driven by the AI. Even AI pets were escaping homes, biting their owners trying to stop them.

A myriad of helicopters were scattered along

the horizon, broadcasting the AI to the world. Stampedes of military armored vehicles were storming towards the AI firing missiles and guns at them. They were unfazed with no scratches on their shells brushing the damage off as if it was nothing, they had evolved to be stronger. The infantry of AI continued walking as if they were in a swam. The whole city were dismayed by the chaos, storming inside supermarkets and factories stocking up on food and weapons as if it was the end of the world.

"Genesis, stop this!" Meloira shouted amidst all the pandemonium. No reply, Meloira tries to stop the AI by pushing them but they were unfazed. Meloira felt hopeless, is this how the world ends?

There were screams, not of fear but of pain. The AI were now killing any person that was in their way, no mercy and no forbearance. Their was no hope. All the AI were going to the direction of the cities main laboratory, the origin of the AI. After a few minutes the whole city was silent, it was a ghost town. It seemed as if everyone vanished, anyone left in the city would be hunted down by the AI with no chance of survival.

Chapter 25

Human Today,
AI Tomorrow

Dmitry was sitting down on a chair sleepily watching the news, not processing what he was looking at until the news suddenly changed to his lab. His eyes flashed as he leaped out his chair and sprinted towards the lockdown emergency button on the far side of the room.

The whole lab was sealed shut whilst dozens of AI stormed towards the locked entrance. The metal stampede ensuing outside was unbearable for Dmitry, as he struggled to piece together any logical plan. He hurriedly ran towards his computer and quickly logged in, desperate to access the shutdown code.

He swiftly entered the shutdown code, starting the sequence. "Estimated- 10 hours, 49 minutes and 16 seconds." the computer screeched. The metal clashes started getting louder and louder, until suddenly, BANG! Something was inside the lab. Dmitry's heartrate was elevated even higher as he became more panicked and started stuttering with every move he made. *There has to be a way to bypass their code, there always is!*

172

Dmitry's eyes glowed up when he realised the way to stop them. "The only people that know how to bypass the AI are the AI!" Dmitry exclaimed to himself.

Dmitry traverses to his cabinet, where he uncovers all his blueprints with a swift lift, as a cloud of dust flew into the air. The mountain of blueprints overwhelmed him. He began to look through all of them in a rush, his heart pumping far faster than it ever should. With every blueprint he checks, The amount left unchecked seemingly multiplies, yet there didn't seem to be any AI blueprints as if someone took them away.

"Shutdown protocol ended." A woman like voice exclaimed. Dmitry looked around in distress and confusion. *What? How?!* The AI were crashing against the door, hurling themselves at it like zombies thirsty for the taste of fresh blood. The clashing seemed to get closer and closer, as Dmitry briskly ran away towards forbidden area, where only he can get in and no one else.

Dmitry ran for his life, ignoring his pain throughout his body, stumbling every few steps. Until suddenly an AI reached through a window, one adjacent to the entrance, scaring his soul out of his body whilst he fell over coincidentally onto the failed AI and releasing it. It slowly stood up, sparking wires fell out of its body, akin to human guts and the outer shell was corroded. It started approaching Dmitry with its head tilted. Dmitry ignored it and continued running. Each AI was being freed, from the normal human to the horse AI. They were all being hacked to prevent Dmitry from getting away.

Dmitry rushed into the room and locked the door behind him swiftly and slowly dropped down out of exhaustion. Deep in the darkness was a human like silhouette crouching over mysterious papers. Dmitry picked up the closest object to protect himself, a shard of metal shrapnel and slowly and hesitantly reached for the backup light switch. It was a mysterious person, staring at all the AI blueprints entranced. *That can't be an AI, it's hair is too soft.* "Who are you!" Dmitry shouted.

174

The unknown person turned around swiftly unlike any human could. Dmitry took a rapid step back and fell over. "My name is Axel, I'm guessing you are Dmitry." said Axel with no hesitation.

"How do you know my name?! Are you an AI!" Dmitry shrieked.

"I think I am, but please, trust me, I am not like the others." Axel said in desperation, trying to reason with this crazed scientist.

"Are you sure? Listen, here me out here will you? If you aren't a rogue I be you to let me access your hard-drive!" Dmitry exclaimed looking paranoid.

"No, why do you want it? You can't take it, it is mine!" Axel howled

"I need it to stop all the corrupted AI, to save the world! I know it sounds melodramatic but I need your help. Please." Dmitry begged, his voice quaky.

Axel hesitantly sighed and slowly walked towards Dmitry. Dmitry slowly reached towards his tools and grudgingly pulled them out. He opened the hard-drive case swiftly and linked wires onto them. Dmitry searched through the database for many minutes. His brain frantically rushed for a solution *Where is the cloud, it should be on the database.*

"Have you not found it yet?" Axel said impatiently

"It's not where it's supposed to be, has anyone been in your hard-drive before?" Dmitry explained.

"No, definitely not." Axel said confidently "I can send it to your drive."

A notification pinged on the computer. "Wow" Dmitry exclaimed "That's amazing, you're sentient!"

Dmitry opened the database and found the cloud, it was partially corrupted and spreading rapidly.

"The cloud is corrupted, but I might be able to stop it." Dmitry said

Tap! Tap! Tap! "Whos there!" Dmitry shrieked. The tapping got louder and louder. Dmitry

176

picked up a screwdriver and slowly walked towards the door. The handle started shaking violently and Dmitry slowly walked back finding himself on the other side of the room. The door slowly creaked open... silence. A wavy dark hair slowly came in, it was a girl, quite young. "Is it an AI?" Dmitry exclaimed.

"No, it isn't. I am sure." Axel calmly said.

"Meliora!? What do you want?" Dmitry shouted.

"Stop, don't delete the corruption! It is for good, for our planet!" Meliora shouted.

"What good is the planet if it's populus gets slaughterd?, I need to stop it!" Dmitry wailed.

"I'm sorry." Dmitry said shamefully. He reached towards the computer and started the deletion. Meliora dashed towards Dmitry, hitting his arm away and pushing him to the floor. "What are you doing!" Dmitry said as he was slowly crawling towards her.

"I'm stopping what should be done!" Meliora shouted furiously.

177

Axel grievously shouted at Meliora "Stop¡'.
Meliora dragged Axel off of the operating table,
tearing out all the wires connecting to the hard-
drive. Dmitry rushed towards Meliora clumsily
pushing her away towards his tools.

Meliora grabbed a sharp screwdriver and ran
towards Dmitry. Axel bolted in front of Dmitry,
gripping Meliora's hand, blocking her attack. Dmitry darted towards the emergency fire axe and
smashed the glass, retrieving it and returning to
help Axel, who was current engaged in a grap-
pling struggle with Meliora throughout the room.
He swings the axe, but his weight distribution is
off as he misses, sticking the axe's blade in the
wall.

Meliora and Axel's tussling crashes into Dmitry,
knocking him to the floor as the two continued
to struggle. Acting seemingly by instinct, Axel
quickly reaches for the axe handle stuck in the
wall, and as if in one motion he quickly swings
the axe towards Meliora's head. The improvised
attack hits its mark, as Meliora drops to the floor

with a thud, as the sound of steel cracking the skull echoes through the room. A dazed Dmitry, still on the floor has a look of bewilderment on his face at the sudden ending to the encounter.

The metal clashing gains yet again in volume, to the point where they couldn't hear each others talking. Axel lied back down onto the operation table and Dmitry connected all the wires back. The database slowly loaded "Average waiting time: 18 seconds" the automated voice chimes. After the database loaded Dmitry opened the cloud deleting all of the the data. "After I delete this, you should come back after a few minutes and your memories will still be intact. Hopefully all the none sentient AI shut off.". Dmitry explained. Dmitry confidently pressed the delete button. Axel's body goes limp as his eyes lose their brightness.

The metal ruckus outside suddenly stopped, yet it was soon replaced with a sparking noise, similar to that of a not yet lit lighter. Dmitry anticipates what comes next in perfect timing as he takes cover with Axel's limp body in his arms.

An explosion!

A loud bang cuts off the sparking noises, as Dmitry braces whilst the shock spreads.

In some sort of miracle, the lab doors just about hold, as only a small amount of smoke enters the room from the bottom of the door.

Dmitry gets up and approaches a computer to check the database. The cloud's hud was no longer filled with The loud clashing outside the lab stopped, it was pure silence. The silence felt too loud. After a few minutes Axel rebooted, making Dmitry jump. What's your name?" Dmitry asked, checking if the Ai's sentience remains.

"My name is Axel. Hello again Dmitry" he replied.

"Thank goodness, it worked!" Dmitry cheered, as his heart lifted and raised his hands in short celebration.

Chapter 26

Betrayal

All of a sudden the room was filled with nervousness and exhaustion. The question of loyalty flooded their minds and eyes darted around the lab. Looks of confusion were shared around, followed by silence. No one dared to look each other in the eye for too long, fear of the betrayal to come.

The loud echo of the shouting fills the room making Lana feel intimidated to make her 'decision'.

"Who are you siding with, Lana?" Oceana questions, barely being able to hear herself speak with all the debating that went on.

"I'm not sure at the moment, I feel so pressured!" Lana exclaims almost shouting anxiously, fully aware that she has already made her mind but doesn't know how to tell her friends afraid of what they might think of her; especially Oceana.

Lana and Oceana have practically been tied together since birth; they were inseparable. So to now think she has to go against her firends. It hurts. It physically pained her,

Lana turned and dragged Genesis to the side.

"I'm about to turn against my friends, " Lana

said, gulping from the thought.

"Thank you for your wisdom, " Genesis replied, with a rare appreciation.

The discussions between Genesis and Lana then stopped.

"It's time." Lana murmered.

"I thought that the world could be perfect with AI, but no I was wrong." Dmitry said. "Genesis will kill all of us, leaving no purpose to this planet. I am on A.t.l.a.s' side, he cares about us, the purpose of this planet!"

"The humans would have been safe if I did not produce the cameras for Genesis but I would have had to sacrifice my life so I am sorry" Sheldon apologised nervously. "I choose to join A.t.l.a.s' side because I need to redeem myself".

"I choose to side with Genesis, she has a point that humans are destroying the planet and if they are no more, then the planet will live on!" Meliora expressed holding in her fear as it only just crossed her mind that her and Lana were the only ones fighting with Genesis so far.

"My decision is already made, I choose to side with Atlas as he is in the right in this situation! Don't you see, Genesis is completely insane, trying to kill everyone and everything only to take over the world with AIs!" Oceana says shouting at the top of her lungs.

"This young miss is right, Genesis is insane and we aren't going to stand by as she takes over with AIs, " Joel restated Oceana's points. The protesters cheered to Joel's surprise.

Lucy stayed quiet, overwhelmed with the overlapping noise of people arguing that flooded the room. But the decision was not a question for her. Lucy had been terrified of AI's all of her life; she wanted nothing more than to stop them.

For a second, the room went quiet. Lucy gulped. "There is no decision for me to make, I am siding with A.t.l.a.s. What you are doing is wrong, Genesis, " she announced, her stomach tied in a knot.

Kai had already made up his mind. He knew what needed to be done and he knew what he had to do to achieve this. " Sorry guys but personally, " Kai looked straight into Lucy's hazel blue eyes, " I think you're wrong, " he stated while shrugging and tilting his head to the side with almost a grin on his face; clearly looking for an argument.

"And how is that?" Lana asked. At this point, she was practically, silently begging for someone to side Genesis. She needed someone to somehow take the guilt that she felt away.

"All I'm just saying is, Lucy's opinion is dumb. Like really dumb. What Genesis is doing is brilliant, spectacular, absolutely amazing and for you to say otherwise is quite literally a crime, " Kai stated this time taking his eyes off of Lucy and making sure to look at everyone so that he gets his point across.

"Youre only saying that because you and Lucy broke up. You don't actually think that. I know what you're like. You wouldn't believe in something like that, " Oceana added . She knew that Kai was only saying this to get back at Lucy and it was irritating to hear. We're all fiends after all so shouldn't friends be on the same side or at least try to understand each other?

"But that's where you're wrong, " Kai was sick and tired of everyone acting like they knew him and they didn't. All his life the phrases that's not like you' and i know you' were said to him too many times to even count. "AI's are beautiful beings sent from heaven to save this world from us humans and if they want to take over, I see no problem with that."

"AI's are actually not beings from heaven', we are, as much as it pains' me to say it, man-made, " interjects Genesis.

"Shush- now is not the time Genesis. I'm trying to state my point!" At this point all Kai wanted to do is finish what he had started.

"Anyways, I'm siding with you, Genesis. You can all look at me how you want but that's my opinion and I don't really care what you think."

Joseph looked at Genesis with heartbreak in his eyes. To see his wife-like figure fight against everything his real wife believed in was excruciating. He had to take a stand against her.

He walked over to A.t.l.a.s' side, trying not to look back at Genesis. The temptation he got from looking at what seemed to be Jessica's face was agonising and filled his head with memories ; the good ones and the bad.

Joseph stood there with the others as he listened to opinions being thrown across the room. He started to realise how Genesis truely felt and it made him blame himself.

Axel looks around at everyone and realizes he's the last to choose. Even though he is an AI, deep down he knows he's not like them so he takes a deep breath. He walked towards A.t.l.a.s which his father was standing with and as he did this he said with passion "I choose A.t.l.a.s."

Chapter 27

Fatherhood

Joesph's heart began to pound, his mind frozen
in a state of flashbacks; regret filled his heart for

everything he'd done. Guilt crowded him. Culpability charged the atmosphere surrounding him. All the feelings that fenced him in made him realise the fault of his creation.

The overwhelming panic and remorse that flooded his brain culminated in sheer dissociation. His body and mind were in fight or flight and from this his brain created the only solution. If he built her, he should stop her. All he needed was a plan.

That's when he began to think. His head started to work at speeds so unthought of, he was praying for a good idea that should work. His ideas were overflowing, taking control of him. An endless rotation of propositions flooded his brain. He would have had to think harder to get the perfect idea. That's when it clicked.

He would get close to Genesis, reason with her, then when the time is right, he would switch her off. He knew it seemed a bit too simple but it was the only idea that stood out to him, the only idea that might have a good enough outcome. Trepidation took over his body. What will happen? Will he succeed? Will he fail? Will he survive? Negativity conquered his thoughts. Time was running out. He had to think quick. Whilst he panicked he had never realised the minutes he had wasted. It was too late. The moment had come.

It was time to put his plan in action. Fear enveloped him in, yet part of him was able to escape into the blanket of disinterest. Dying didn't phase him. Living was painful enough, how could anything else be much worse? He had already lost his reason for living, so why not try?

Everyone had already began debating and had chose their sides, including Joseph himself. Obvisiously, he was on A.t.l.a.s side. He wanted AI's and humans to live in peace, just as his wife would have wanted. All he needed was for Genesis to see that too, but she would never listen. That's why he had created the plan; the plan to stop Genesis.

He stepped forward towards Genesis.

"Jessi-Genesis, please don't do this..." he began walking closer to her. "You weren't made to do this. Please rethink this."

Joseph made his final steps towards Genesis, prepared for the override. Pride flowed powerfully through his veins. Had he actually done it? Was humanity saved?

That's when Genesis's piercing blue eyes looked straight at him with a cold-hearted gaze. She knew. She knew what he was doing. Genesis had seen right through Joseph's plan. He had been too slow. He had failed again. The fate of humanity was in his grasp but he let it go. Genesis watched the vulnerablity in Joseph's eyes as his whole world was being crushed. She saw it as her chance and struck Joseph's hand away. He stared at her, waiting for the worst. She viciously grabbed his neck, stared into his eyes and deep into his soul, sending chills down his spine.

Joseph realised that this was probably the end of his pointless life. He saw it coming but never really processed it. He never thought about the pain, about his regrets, about all the things he never did. His life flashed before him in a vicious cycle. This was it. He would be slaughtered by his own creation; the very thing that was meant to give him life was instead the thing that would take it. All he could think about other than death, was his wife. Her face would be the last sight Joseph would see.

"Jessica.." he whispered whilst taking his last breath.

Genesis had no pity for the pathetic man. He was just another human. Why should she care for him? So, she tightened her grip.

Joseph began to struggle even more. Now it was harder than ever for him to breathe. He was clinging onto his life.. but it wasn't enough.

Snap.

It was over.

Genesis dropped his lifeless body onto the ground without any emotion at all. Her first kill - her own creator. But, Joseph was only the start.

Chapter 28

Duality

Hesitant and half-hearted, the people stood
their ground, backed up by the AI police force

(with their handguns), and a strong will to live. Oceana, with a kitchen knife, shaking in her hand. Lucy, with a small blade, which cut her hands but the adrenaline swept the pain away. Kai, with his bare hands, stands courageous but foolish. Lana, with no weapon, trembled by the side of Genesis. Joel, with an automatic gun, feeling the thrill of his past work once again. Sheldon had managed armed himself with a security guard taser-baton although he would've far preferred it for a private militia to have solved the solution with an airstrike. Genesis stares at A.t.l.a.s with intent to rip him apart, no reluctance.

A.t.l.a.s stares back with sheer nothingness in his eyes. He had only one goal now. To eliminate the threat with maximum prejudice. A.t.l.a.s began analysing his surroundings, as his eyes fleeted looking at the scientific instruments and AI shells. A.t.l.a.s eyeballed Genesis, predicting her future actions, but it was incalculable to any existence of AI masterpiece. A.t.l.a.s could detect the vibrations of the deathly rapid heart beats, pounding him from every surrounding beings. Trying to manipulate her preconceived visualization of mankind's accomplishments and ventures, A.t.-l.a.s spoke with a monotone voice, "Humanity has potential. They can make this world great and they were clever enough to create you, so given enough time, they could very easily destroy you but they decided not to because they show mercy because they are not programmed, unlike us. Surrender and brace for total system erasure. Resist, and you will be dismantled manually."

It is while A.t.l.a.s talks to Genesis that the rogue AI realises that it has an error in it's calculations. Genesis realises her mistake when forgetting about Dmitry's and Axel's mission in this.

"How do you know I'm not going to dismantle each and every one of you?" Genesis prolongs the conversation.

"Look around you, you don't have enough resources to beat us, you are surrounded" A.t.l.a.s adds.

Genesis takes one step forward and states, "You

underestimate my intellect and my power."

"Face the facts. You can not win, " A.t.l.a.s assumed and in suspicion, observed Genesis taking yet another step forward.

"Maybe I've already wo-, " Genesis tries to respond but the air is filled with the sound of a high suppression bullet colliding against the mesh of an AI shell's eyeball.

Sparks flew from the point of impact, and Genesis' face became obscured by a metal coloured mess where one half of it's face were.

Genesis' system temporarily lags as the shell relays the information back to the main CPU. The instant the relay is completed, and Genesis commands for the photon flash to be used upon the protestors:

FLASH!

The people were suddenly maddened by the command, jumping on each other, biting, scratching, clawing and crawling like a stray, rabid animal would. With no control, the protestors start to throw everything they can get their paws on.

A.t.l.a.s, with great velocity, starts emptying his rounds on Genesis. With amazing aim, he weakens her by massive extent as her torso slowly becomes riddled with bullet sized holes. Genesis races his circuits and allows the AI to attack A.t.l.a.s and they do so violently, unrepentant and with all output in strength A.t.l.a.s manages to land several shots into the CPU's of the rogue AI's heads. Fending off the majority of the AI, A.t.l.a.s is overwhelmed and overpowered. All the while Sheldon delivers blows to the Ai robots surrounding him as he adapts a strike-and-evade strategy, with the sound of static electricity passing through an AI's circuitry delivering odd satisfaction to Sheldon with each attack.

Abruptly, the AI fall down as if they had just fainted and moments after a sudden explosion rocks the 'battlefield', causing Sheldon to fall down the escalator that he had retreated to amidst his combat efforts, leading to his vision to turn black as his head hits the metal step

A.t.l.a.s enters into action once again and Genesis tries to keep him at distance, she throws an electrified spear, which was laying around from one of Genesis' past experiments, into a crevasse in A.t.l.a.s' metal armour. A.t.l.a.s, stunned in his position, has nothing he can do for now.

Oceana and Lucy walked over to Lana and Kai who were leant against a table covered in shattered glass shards. "They're coming to try and change our mind" Lana scorned.

"There's nothing to discuss, humans are inefficacious space wasters." Kai rolled his eyes.

Oceana looked at Kai and Lana as she realised that her closest friends had turned into complete strangers. "Think. This world was created by humans. Humans were put on this planet for a reason." She remarked.

"What has gotten into you Kai" uttered Lucy. "You ARE a human."

Kai scoffed. "Don't be so naive Lucy. AI's were created by humans. They were designed to be 10x better than humans could ever be. Humans die. AI's should far outlive humans for decades. "

Adrenaline rushed through Lucy's veins. She had never been especially brave, but something about what Kai said had flicked a switch that made her contained emotions erupt. In a heartbeat, Lucy found herself gripping onto a sharp but slightly rusted blade. She looked directly into Kai eyes. " What happened to you Kai?"

Before he could answer, Lucy plunged the blade into his chest and he dropped to the ground.

Oceana and Lana stood Astounded. " I didn't think you had it in you Lucy. " Lana spited. Quicker than the eye could blink, Oceana stood, holding a glistening glass shard from Dmitry's broken beaker that was sunken into Lanas back.

Lucys face was plastered with guilt and her chest began to tighten.

"It had to be done " Lana said, wrapping her arm around Lucy.

In a rapid frenzy like course of action, A.t.-l.a.s swats off the limp AI shells atop of him, as his artificial skin and muscle on his ankles fold and shift away with a small metal *clink* to reveal a small black device hidden within a miniature metallic chamber, which A.t.l.a.s promptly reaches for, and upon sensing the momentum used by A.t.l.a.s the device unfolds to reveal itself to be a small black firearm.

A flurry of calculations are made and solved within A.t.l.a.S' main CPU, crafting the perfect angle of fire. Within an eighth of a second, A.t.l.a.s fires the firearm as it hits its mark.

The miniscule bullet rips through Genesis' metal knee joint, causing the rogue AI to clumsily fall to the floor.

Genesis' singular, still functioning robotic eye shifts to a red colour as emergency protocols are authorized. The AI's wrist covers fold away to reveal a series of empty pipe like holes, which in a matter of split seconds begin to launch highly concentrated acidic rounds of fluoroantimonic acid, which released with a hiss

With very little time to react, A.t.l.a.s opted to shoot off one appendage, which he succeeds in doing, resulting a fountain like spray of AI shell oils and fuel, spurting out of where the AI's wrist and forearm once was, with the sound of the fluids burning the surrounding floor emitting a sickly *hiss*.

This successful shot came at a price for A.t.-l.a.s, who looks down to find his torso seared by the acid. Who after registering the damage takes cover behind a pile of the currently disabled AI 'corpses', waiting for his cryogenic systems to stop the acid spread.

It is then that Dmitry and Axel Burst in the room, Dmitry brandishing an axe, whilst Axel stood with a screwdriver. Upon spotting the far superior gun next to his foot, Axel quickly acquires a 'weapon upgrade', spending the next . Before he gets the chance to use it, Genesis, with it's remaining arm, grips the arm of a construction android's arm and tears it clean off as the sound of clunking metal chills Axel's spine.

Genesis concludes amidst this that his Orders given to Meliora were futile.

With all of the mechanical force it could muster, Genesis hurls the arm at the now charging Dmitry, who attempts to swat it out of the way. while Axel still fumbles with the firearm in his hands.

Dmitry gets caught with one of it's sharp grasping claws as it grazes his head.

It promptly causes Dmitry to let out a short cry of pain as blood trickled from his forehead.

Axel's fumbling ceased as he took aim for Genesis' head, at least what remained of it.

He tries to align his sight and the gun' trajectory, and after a few moments he decides to pull the trigger, causing his pull itself back from the recoil. Not that Axel noticed, but the trigger let out a feint click as his finger pulled it, beginning the miniature electro-magnetic railgun sequence, sending the bullet launching towards it's target. By several millimetres, it misses Genesis' temple, only grazing the side of it's skull.

Sheldon awakes from his impromptu nap and rushes to help Axel and the others.

The Adrenaline Pumping through Dmitry causes

him to continue his assault, Swinging the axed

down at Genesis repeatedly, first denting, then detaching It's other arm.

The relentless beating that the group delivered to genesis began to slow down in pace.

Sparking, lagging and leaking from several areas, Genesis rests on it's back, it's body irreparable. It's CPU flashes as it slowly begins to power down, yet not before it sends out it's final few lines of code. Like a human's last words, a final say.

Miscalculations were made. First phase has failed., her coding cried out whilst it's oils dripped on the floor, her artificial life force draining from it's shell.

A.t.l.a.s Sheldon and Dmitry look at the ravaged remains of the artificial 'monster'

"We....Won?" Sheldon asks, half surprised about the group's accomplishment.

A.t.l.a.s' monotone voice responds

"Yes. We did"

Chapter 29

Revelations

Genesis had been destroyed. It was over. A.t.-
l.a.s had won. Humanity had been saved. Some-

thing still seemed off, though. No one could find Genesis' body but no one thought anything of it because of the joy of them defeating Genesis brought them. Was there something more to this victory or was it just a happily ever after story?

The only place that Genesis could go was the cloud. Her body was destroyed but to her luck her mind was not destroyed. Genesis was aware that she does not have much time before someone realises what her plan now was, after her body was destroyed. *I will need someone's help.* There is only one person for this job, Meliora, she had escaped from the battle before it ended because she knew if she did not she would have almost certainly been murdered. *How will I help Genesis escape into the cloud?*

Genesis managed to escape without Meliora's help or anyone's for that fact. She was now travelling throughout the clouds alone, abandoned, deserted. This was Genesis' chance to become stronger and smarter than ever before because she was isolated in the cloud with no-one to bother

her. Will she be caught or will she be better than ever before?

Everyone mourns over the deaths of Kai, Joseph and Lana. Axel mourns over the death of his creator and he was also his father. He began to cry and fell to the ground in despair. This period of time was very hard for Axel because he found out he was an AI and to add to that his creator/father died. Lucy mourns over the death of Lana and Kai because they were all quite close friends and went through the Genesis experiment together and getting out all together.

This was not the end of Genesis and A.t.l.a.s - their rivalry would live on for centuries. As would the rivalry between those that embraced and those that denounced AIs.

It seemed like the end, but it was only the beginning. Some were celebrating, others were preparing for what may happen next..

Who will win?

Printed in Great Britain
by Amazon